Hot Flashes and Hockey Slashes

HOT FLASH HOOKUPS
BOOK ONE

MARIKA RAY

SYLVIE STEWART

Hot
Flashes
and
HOCKEY
SLASHES

Description

He's a hot, shirtless hockey player...and he's my fake date for my ex-husband's wedding. Talk about a hot flash to beat all hot flashes.

The wedding bells are ringing and my ex-husband is the groom! When my grown kids hook me up with a fake date to my ex-hubby's tropical island nuptials, I expect sun, sand, and plenty of fruity cocktails - not steamy nights with a shirtless pro hockey player!

Roman might be all swagger on the ice, but this growly, egotistical male model of perfection has a soft side too. While I battle dresses made for twenty-somethings, awkward run-ins with my ex, and unwelcome hot flashes, Roman is there to distract me with flirty compliments, stay up late with me when I can't sleep, and make me feel vibrant and ageless.

As good as it feels, none of this is real, and Roman is *way* out of my league. Who's going to believe this gorgeous, famous, muscle-bound athlete would ever date a scatter-brained, hot flashing, insomniac nerd with twenty stubborn extra pounds around the middle?

But as the big day approaches, we grow closer. Wedding activities lead to beach walks at sunset, and his oh-so-talented fingers twist my hormones up in a whole new way. Gazing into Roman's eyes, I start to wonder if he could be my shot at a real happily ever after.

That's the thing about vacations, though; at some point, you need to return to reality.

Chapter One

Olivia

"How long does it take to dig a six-foot hole?" I swipe a hand over my sweaty forehead, not even caring that I likely smeared garden soil across my face.

Evie doesn't hesitate. "Six feet wide or six feet deep?"

"Both," I bark into the phone as I attempt to light the envelope in my hand on fire through some telepathic transfer of molten fury from my eyeballs. *He's got some nerve!*

"Shit," my best friend replies. There's no need to ask whom I'm preparing to use as garden fertilizer. "What did he do?"

Channeling serenity from the early spring sky and its accompanying breeze across my skin, I raise my eyes from the envelope and draw in a deep breath. It doesn't work. "He invited me to his wedding," I cough out before exhaling and finishing through gritted teeth, "In Belize. I didn't even know he was engaged!"

Evie gasps with a degree of indignation that proves why she's my very best friend. "I'm on my way. You got an extra shovel, or should I bring my own?"

Twenty minutes later, I've abandoned my garden tools and the rest of the mail as Evie and I sit across from one another at my kitchen table. The cursed invitation with its luscious ivory parchment and hand-calligraphed swirls rests on the surface between us where we watch it like it might morph into a snapping crocodile at any moment.

"Why would he even want me there?" I'm not mad my ex is moving on, believe me; I'm just pissed this is how he chose to tell me. So help me God, if he's telling the kids the same way, I might actually go through with the fertilizer plan.

A bead of residual sweat drips down my cleavage, and I pluck my shirt from my chest to provide some ventilation. Evie hits the switch for the overhead fan, and I sigh in appreciation. It's not her first day as my hot flash wing-woman.

"He doesn't expect you to actually show," she reassures, slender hands cradling her coffee mug and vigilant brown eyes still waiting for a flash of crocodile teeth. "The guy can't stand that you've become wildly successful without him, so he's looking for something to rub in your face."

I choke out a laugh. If he could only see me now in all my sweaty glory, an extra twenty pounds having parked itself around my middle and the bags under my eyes big enough to store a set of keys and some extra change. He honestly shouldn't have bothered.

I've heard about divorced couples who remain friends —best friends, even—but it's safe to say Scott and I won't be exchanging friendship bracelets or braiding one another's hair anytime soon.

Not that we aren't *friendly*, mind you. In fact, we're nothing but smiles when we see one another.

Like the smile I sent Scott across the table at Dylan's twenty-first birthday dinner when our son mentioned that his dad's latest girlfriend thought Dylan's anthropology major meant he'd be working at Anthroplogie after graduation.

Or the smile Scott sent me over Holly's high school graduation cake last spring as he handed our daughter a set of keys to a brand new convertible. Never mind we'd already settled on a plane ticket to Spain as our shared gift.

For the benefit of our kids, Scott and I are the masters of friendly, cordial, and polite on the few occasions a year we're required to see each other. I simply hadn't anticipated his surprise wedding to a woman I've never heard of to be one of them—and in Central America, no less.

I slide my untouched coffee aside. It smells divine, but the caffeine will only make the sweating worse. "Well, considering I haven't been on a date since the divorce and my lady cave condition is only hospitable to cacti, I'm willing to concede. Do I include a white flag with the congratulatory card or does he expect me to actually fawn all over . . ." I tilt my head to read the admittedly beautiful script. "Taylor?"

Evie sets down her cup and finally relaxes back into one of my cross-back chairs, her long midnight hair spilling over one shoulder. "What does it say about me that I kind of want to meet her?"

"It says you're human." I manage a grin as the fan does its work and the heat in my cheeks begins to subside. "And considering there's undoubtedly an identical envelope waiting in your mailbox, you may soon get your chance." Her husband *is* Scott's best friend, after all.

Her lip curls. "I'm not going to that rat bastard's wedding. Dan can go on his own for all I care." Her eyes widen then, back snapping straight. "You don't think Scott's going to start expecting Dan and me to do *couple* things with them, do you?"

I rest my elbow on the table, dropping my chin into my hand as I give her *the look*. The same look I've been perfecting since the day I filed for divorce and our mutual friends all felt the need to "choose." It takes Evie only a nanosecond to recognize it and roll her eyes.

Still, I feel the need to reiterate, especially at a time like this. "I love you to pieces for always having my back, but this divorce is between Scott and me. You and Dan have known us for two decades; there's no reason to choose."

"Well, Dan still adores you, as you well know. But I also won't be surprised if he's put on best-man duty. I'll never understand my husband's taste in men—even if his taste in women is on point." She grins, and I know she's heard me, so I don't launch into the part of the speech about Scott surely having *some* redeeming qualities if I managed to stay married to him for almost twenty years. "But I'm still not going."

I lift my abandoned coffee cup and clink it to hers. "That makes two of us."

Since work doesn't miraculously do itself, Evie and I part ways to get on with our days. Owning my own company has its perks—like calling my own hours—but it also makes me responsible for the livelihoods of almost fifty other people.

Decisions I make have consequences, and I don't take that lightly.

So I settle in at the big white scrolled desk in my home

office and use the remote to switch on the mini split resting high on one wall. A/C in March? You bet your ass.

One benefit of my full afternoon of meetings and emails is that I'm too busy to spare even one more thought for Scott and his scheme to mess with my head. There are operations issues and production schematics that take precedence over my ex and his swinging dick show.

But when my phone rings a couple hours later and I see Holly's name on the screen, all my bravado crumbles.

Shit. Please, God, let Scott have used the brain above his belt for once.

"Hey, sweetie." My tone borders on cartoonish when I answer.

"Mom, oh my god. This is so exciting!"

My shoulders slump in relief at the elation in my daughter's voice. He didn't tell her yet—either that, or she hasn't checked her dorm mailbox yet today.

I swivel my chair to face the large picture window that looks over my backyard, but before I can gather myself to inquire about the source of her enthusiasm, she barrels on, "He said they planned it to coincide with Dylan's and my spring break—and we each get to bring a friend! Isn't that so cool? Hannah's already shopping for bikinis online. Belize is *way* better than Myrtle Beach!" She lets out a squeal while my brain trips over itself on its attempt to process this information.

"So, you're okay?" I rock forward in the chair, a torrent of emotions tearing through me. Relief at my daughter's emotional wellbeing, gratitude that Scott didn't screw this up, and—okay, I can admit it—a tiny dash of petty resentment that my kid doesn't appear to be batting an eye about her father getting remarried so suddenly.

"*Okay?* I'm over the moon! And Hannah and I both

agree you are pure class for coming too. I gotta say I was worried how you might take the news, but as usual, you are a rock star. Looks like I had nothing to worry about!"

Oh god. Oh no. My hand itches for that shovel again, and I shoot to my feet.

"That's sweet, Holls, but—"

She cuts me off. "Dylan's super psyched you're coming too. He said he hasn't seen you since Christmas. How is that possible?"

My vision clouds over, the backyard disappearing from view and my voice coming out almost hollow. "He's been busy with school and—" I get cut off again by the whirling dervish that is my spawn.

"I can't wait for us to go snorkeling together—the reefs are supposed to be amazing, and Dad and Taylor have all these events planned. It's going to be straight fire."

Blinking to clear my head, I decide it's time to nip this in the bud before she announces I've apparently volunteered myself to perform the ceremony uniting Scott and his child bride.

Okay, now I'm just being bitchy. I don't know the first thing about this woman.

"Sweetie, it sounds great, and I'm thrilled for you that you're going. I'm just not sure if I can make it." Possible excuses ricochet off the walls of my skull while my daughter's declaration of my "rock star" status bats them away.

"Of course you can. Ashley can practically run the business on her own if her Insta posts are anything to go by. Did you know the paps caught Jennifer Aniston wearing your Livvies?"

"Paps?" I'm certain it's a word I should know, but I've never claimed to be trendy. The fact that I own my own fashion brand is something I find to be the height of comedy on an almost daily basis.

"Paparazzi, Mom." I can almost hear her eye roll. "Hannah has been telling everyone on campus that her roommate's mom is the famous brain behind the hottest shoes in Hollywood."

I don't know that I would go that far, but a spark of pride blooms in my chest nevertheless. I may be far from a fashion maven or a clothes horse, but two years ago, I somehow managed to make a name for myself when a pair of bespoke sandals I produced on a whim with a 3D printer captured the attention of some very influential people. It was nothing but dumb luck, but I've been riding the wave ever since—with the help of my very social-media-savvy assistant, Ashley, that is.

"Well, tell Hannah we'll get her a pair when we can get a scan of her foot." Hannah is a doll, and the two of them are so close, it's hard to believe they only met six months ago when student housing paired them up as roommates.

I hear a rustling sound over Holly's muffled voice. "My mom says she's going to get you a pair of Livvies." A scream reverberates through the line before Holly comes back on, laughing in my ear.

"It's not work that's standing in the way, Holly." I don't want to lie to her. "It's just a bit... awkward." Although hanging out with my kids in paradise doesn't sound terribly taxing. I miss those goobers.

"I totally hear you," she responds, much to my relief— proving that honesty truly is the best policy. "Hannah and I have already thought about that, and we're getting you a date for the wedding."

"A date!? No, that's not what I meant," I rush to halt whatever interfering plans my daughter and her bestie might be hatching. The only thing worse than showing up to your ex-husband's wedding alone and looking a hot mess is showing up with a hired escort from a local Belizean street corner. Good god.

She continues as if I haven't spoken, "I mean, I know you and Dad are super chill with each other, but no woman wants to show up to her ex's wedding flying solo, right?"

Oh, dear god.

"No! It's fine, really!" What the hell am I saying? "It will be great being there on my own—a vacation suite to myself sounds like heaven." *Get a grip, Olivia!* "And I've always wanted to visit Belize." *What?* I'm quite certain the thought has never crossed my mind.

"Oh, shoot. We're gonna be late for class! Gotta run. Love you, Mom!"

The line goes dead, and I'm left with a phone dangling from my hand and a problem the size of New Jersey to figure out.

<h1 style="text-align:center">Chapter Two</h1>

Roman

"You're the last guy here, Roman. Trying to make the rest of us look bad?"

I open one eye while keeping my jaw locked together. Banks, my best friend and teammate on the Florida Storm Chasers, is standing by the tank of ice water I'm currently submerged in, looking fresh as a fucking daisy while I can't decide what hurts more, my knee or my hamstring.

"Doesn't take much," I drawl in opposition to the utter agony of having my entire body submerged in freezing water.

"Fuck off," Banks shoots back, leaning in and looking at my cell phone on the table next to the tank. Nosy motherfucker. "Your mommy called."

"Don't you have a woman somewhere to seduce?"

Banks is almost as old as me and just as single. But not quite as old, as he likes to frequently point out. Among other illustrious awards over the years, I hold the title of oldest professional hockey player in the league, a fact that wakes me up at night when I really could use the beauty sleep. That and the constant pain my body is in these days. Didn't help that some jackwagon decided to use his stick on my kneecap instead of the puck end of last season. Fucker got ejected from the game for the slashing violation, but I got a lifetime injury.

"Nah, I just need to stroll into the club and they swarm."

I shake my head in disgust and go back to my measured breathing. Two more minutes and I can get out of the tank and head home for some grub. Tonight's game was an asskicker. All was going great until Smithie on the Night-Owls decided to slam me up against the boards because he didn't like how I stole the puck from him. Not my fault even an old guy is faster than him. Thank god I didn't hear a crack when I hit, but my shoulder started screaming and didn't let up the rest of the game.

"Oh, and a text from Hannah Banana too. You're Mr. Popular."

That has my eyes shooting open. I surge up out of the water, unconcerned about the five-minute goal I didn't hit in the ice water. Snatching the phone off the table and away from Banks's prying eyes, I check the screen. Sure enough, there's a text from my daughter, Hannah. She's off at college in North Carolina, probably very happy to be geographically farther away from her father. We've had a patchy relationship, mostly because I'm an immature asshole with a job that has me on the road most of the year. Plus, females. They're mysteries, man.

"Dude, put some pants on. Shrinkage is real." Banks

throws a towel at me and blocks my view of what Hannah wrote.

I smirk at him and shimmy my hips for good measure. I may be old, but I still got it. Shrinkage, my ass. Banks snickers and I use the towel to blot the icy drops on my skin. Holding the phone high, I squint to read what Hannah texted.

> Hannah: Can you call me when you get a chance? I have a favor to ask.

I nearly bobble the phone. She wants me to call her? After I missed Parent Day at her university back in the fall, I haven't been able to get her on the phone at all. She'll shoot me a single-word text every few weeks as proof of life, but an actual conversation? Must be my lucky fucking day.

"Hey, how is Hannah?" Banks is looking over my shoulder and it's creeping me out.

I shrug away from him and shoot him a look that would have most men cowering if they knew what was good for them. "Why the fuck do you want to know?"

Banks shrugs. "You know that kid I was mentoring last summer? He goes to App State now."

Far as I knew, App State only had a club hockey team. Nothing anyone talked about. I wrap the towel around my waist and move over to the lockers to grab my clothes. Most of the team has left the locker room in shambles after the game, dirty clothes on the floor and wet towels all over the benches. Bunch of slobs. "So?"

"So maybe I should introduce them." Banks follows like some kind of hound dog looking for a treat.

I spin around and shoot him another glare. "You want

to set my daughter up with a hockey player? Have you lost your fucking mind?"

Banks takes a step back, his hand over his heart like he's shocked. He knows my history with Hannah, and he knows my one regret in life is that I didn't take better care of her when she was younger. Now that she's older and wiser, she sees through my bullshit and holds my feet to the fire. Setting her up with a hockey player would be the last thing she or I would want.

"We're not all assholes, you know."

I throw off the towel and pull on my trousers and collared shirt. The press is long gone, but old habits die hard. Never leave a game in plain street clothes. Always dress like the goddamn professionals we're paid ridiculous amounts of money to be. "Ninety-nine percent of us are." I sit on the bench to slide on my Italian leather loafers. "Look, just drop the Hannah thing, okay?"

"Okay, sorry. Just thought it would give you two something to talk about."

I grin smugly. "I don't need the help, man. She just asked me to call her."

Banks whistles. "Well, in that case, I'll leave you to it. See you tomorrow bright and early for practice."

He takes off and I'm not far behind him, sliding in behind the wheel of my beloved silver Maserati. I get her flying down the highway away from the arena and closer to my condo in downtown Tampa with a view of the Gulf. Then I put the phone on Bluetooth and call Hannah. When she answers on the first ring, I get the feeling this favor means a lot to her. Of course, I'll give her whatever she needs just to get back in her good graces. What's the point of having stacks of money unless I can shower it on the people I love?

"Dad?"

"Hey, honey. Got your message and called back as soon as I could. What's up?"

"Okay, so I know you have seven days off soon, right?"

I frown, not because I'm not happy to have seven days in a row off during a busy season, but because this is the first year in a long time that I wasn't invited to play in the All Star game. I haven't had those seven days off since my second year in the league. It's yet another blow in a year full of blows.

"Uh, yeah, that's right." Frankly, I'm surprised Hannah knows my schedule. Then again, the kid's bright. Far brighter than me or her mother, one beautiful puck bunny in a long line of puck bunnies. I nearly swerve off the road as an idea occurs to me. "Maybe we could spend–"

"So, I have an idea!" Hannah interrupts over the crackle of the line. "How about you come with me to Belize?"

My heart, the one so banged up and hardened I'm not sure it still operates like a fully functioning organ, jolts in my chest. I throw a fist up in the air in silent victory. "Yes! Definitely." I clear my throat, hoping I don't sound as desperate as I feel. "Sounds good."

Hannah lets out an ear-piercing squeal and I almost join in. "We're going to have so much fun! You're going to love Holly's mom and Holly and even Dylan, though he'd kind of an asshole in only the way a big brother can be, you know?"

I don't have any fucking clue what she's talking about. "Sure, sure."

"So, Holly said the room's already taken care of. I'll text you the hotel name. You should probably get there on Saturday though so you can get to know Holly's mom before you have to show up to the pre-wedding events together."

Warning bells clang in my head as I pull into the underground garage. I lift a hand in greeting to the bored guard and make my way to my assigned parking space. Once the car's in park, I refocus on the conversation.

"Wedding? Holly's mom? What are you talking about, Hannah?"

There's muffled shuffling on the other end of the line before Hannah's back. "Oh, I didn't explain it all very well, did I?"

I shake my head, just happy she's still talking to me. Ecstatic she wants to spend time with me.

"So, you know Holly, right?" I shake my head again, not that she can see me, and she plows on, "She's my very best friend and roommate and her parents are divorced. Her dad's getting remarried in Belize and invited everyone to the wedding. Including Holly's mom. Talk about awkward, right? Holly's mom is rad though. I mean, have you seen Livvies?" Hannah's voice trails off into a squeal again while I try to keep up. "So, anyway, she needs a date."

"Holly?" I mumble, feeling like I'm too old to keep up and hating that feeling.

"No!" Hannah's peal of laughter is like that first sip of cold beer after a tough game. "Holly's *mom* needs a date. She can't show up to her ex's wedding without a date. I mean, the secondhand embarrassment alone would ruin our trip. That's where you come in!"

"Wait, what?" I sit up straight, leaning closer to the speaker where Hannah's voice is coming from. Surely, I can't be hearing her right.

"Yeah. You'll be Holly's mom's date for the wedding

and we can spend the week together in Belize. Everybody wins, right?"

I open my mouth and nothing comes out. I can't say no when I've been begging Hannah to give me even a scrap of her attention. But how can I be someone's blind date at a wedding when the press is sure to get ahold of this and make it something it isn't? This has disaster written all over it. For Hannah's friend's sake, I should say no.

"Please, Daddy?" Hannah begs in that voice that reminds me of when she was little and I'd buy her ice cream, even if it was right before dinner. I caved every fucking time.

I think of all the times I've let her down. All the school performances I missed, the Christmases spent on the road instead of with her, even her senior prom when I planned to be there to assess her date and then missed my flight. I've let Hannah down so many times I'm amazed she still talks to me.

"Yeah, honey. Count me in," I hear myself say.

Hannah squeals and I cringe. "Thank you, Daddy! This is going to be so much fun!"

And then the line goes dead and I slump back against my leather seat. I squeeze my eyes shut against the dull ache in my head. It's nothing compared to the searing pain in my shoulder and the niggle of pain in my hamstring. Seven days in Belize is doable, right? Just show up to a wedding with a strange woman on my arm and then I can spend the other six days with my daughter, lying out in the sunshine and letting my body rest. My physical therapist did just tell me I needed an extended break.

Feeling better about things, I climb out of the car and into the elevator, heading up to my penthouse. The place is exactly how I left it: sterile, cold, and completely devoid of personal effects. I'm just not home long enough to mess it up or bother with decorating. Dumping my duffle bag in the entryway, I grab the one framed photo I do have. It's a picture of me and Hannah from years ago. The bow in her hair is falling out while her little arms wrap around my neck. Our faces are squished together in matching grins.

I have no idea what I just signed myself up for, but for that little girl, I'd do damn near anything.

Chapter Three

Olivia

> Evie: Did I just see you hiding behind a bush?

> Me: No. I'm hiding behind a beautiful Flame of the Woods shrub.

I'm totally hiding behind a bush.

Shoving my phone into my skirt pocket, I shuffle sideways to the cover of another Flame of the Woods, this one tall enough that I can stand upright and take another peek without being exposed.

My immature antics are a necessary evil, seeing as I just stepped into the resort lobby to find Evie and Dan standing in casual conversation with Scott and his bride-to-be. (Obviously, Evie came to Belize. It's a well-known best friend rule that if your BFF is forced to attend the wedding of her ex to prove to her kids that she's not only a rock star but that they are her number-one priority, your ass is going to be there to get her drunk and have her back.)

I am in no condition to meet my ex-husband's gorgeous fiancée—and she absolutely is. She's also young; I'd guess at least ten years younger than my forty-three, but it's hard to be certain through a screen of foliage.

Dammit, I had a plan, and it didn't include cowering behind a plant while my best friend kept my ex distracted.

I was supposed to check into my room early and take a long luxurious bath, after which I'd give myself the works: exfoliating scrub, full-body slather of expensive lotion, jade-roller treatment, mega concealer, dewy makeup designed to make it look like I wake up that way, and multiple swipes of lash-lengthening mascara to have my blue eyes going electric.

Instead, I'm two hours late, having spent ages on the airport tarmac stewing in a ninety-degree flying sardine can with the captain assuring us every five minutes that our gate would be available "any moment." The good news is I likely shed ten pounds in the process by sweating through my clothes.

The sight of a uniformed chauffeur holding a placard bearing my name was heaven on earth, as was the air-conditioned car ride to what I assumed would be the resort. Instead, my suitcase and I were deposited on a dock where a small speedboat waited to whisk me to a key off the coast. I've had worse Saturdays.

One terrifying thirty-minute ride with a boat captain named Sergio who happens to be a huge fan of puns—he was right, by the way; I really couldn't *Belize* my eyes when I saw the resort—and I had achieved an eighties-level hair volume that not even an entire case of Aqua Net could endeavor to accomplish.

And now I'm hiding behind a shrub while the dock valet has absconded with my suitcase and I have no earthly idea where to find my room—or how to get there without alerting Scott and Taylor to my presence.

"This place is gorgeous!" Evie suddenly exclaims, her arms sweeping wide to indicate the breezy opulence of the lobby. I notice one index finger wagging in the direction of a covered walkway leading to what looks like a beach. "I can't believe you put us all up in private bungalows over the water!"

I owe Evie my first born. Looks like Dylan and I have a difficult conversation ahead of us.

Continuing her performance, she grasps Scott's arm. "And you're a peach for putting Olivia right next door! What's our bungalow name again, Dan? The Sea Turtle? So cute!" At this point, I'm guessing the bride is mentally scrambling for how to accommodate a deaf wedding guest at the last minute.

I don't stick around to find out how this riveting drama ends, however, instead taking the opportunity to snatch my purse and laptop bag and race toward the beach.

By the time my sandaled feet hit the hot sand, my breath is coming in pants and I've shed my linen blouse, leaving me in a skin-tight camisole that was never meant to see the light of day. Desperate times and all that, though. The breeze off the water whips my hair into my eyes as I trudge over sand and shells on a hunt for anything indicating the location of The Sea Turtle.

A promising row of neat thatch-roofed structures standing on stilts over the water catches my eye, and I puff my way over a rise of sand to investigate. It's going to be a cold shower instead of a hot bath at this point, but either way my private bungalow is calling my name.

A wood-slatted sign declaring The Angelfish protrudes from the sand, and I hurry by the first bungalow's private pier to determine the names of the other structures. I pass The Humpback—an unfortunate choice, if you ask me—to find The Sea Turtle a dozen yards down the beach. Thank God.

Glancing back to The Humpback, I spy the silhouette of a tall man through the billowing curtains, so I forge ahead, readjusting the heavy laptop bag on my shoulder and scraping a damp tendril of frizzed-out hair from my cheek.

Almost there.

With energy stores of unknown origin, I skip up the wood steps to the private pier of the next bungalow and hurry to the door. Clear turquoise water surrounds me with sparkles of sun reflecting off the calm ripples. Evie wasn't kidding. This place is *gorgeous*.

Reaching for the sliding door handle, I hope against hope that the bellhop already dropped my bags so I can fix the hot mess I'm sure to encounter in the mirror. But I'm startled when I hear voices inside.

"Melissa! I forgot to bring my shampoo in the shower with me. Help a girl out, would you?" a woman shouts from inside.

I must have read the signs wrong. Either that or Evie was mistaken and I'm not in the bungalow next to hers.

Retracing my steps, I summon my last trace of energy as the laptop strap digs into my shoulder and my purse wilts to the sand. The middle bungalow is indeed The Sea Turtle, and another glance confirms that, yes, The Humpback is already occupied. I know this for certain when said occupant slides opens the front door to his bungalow and shouts something my way.

From this distance, all I can tell is that he's tall. So tall, in fact, that he has to duck down to clear the door frame.

I sigh and cup my hands around my mouth. "What?! I can't hear you!"

He starts walking down his pier, long strides eating up the planks as I drag my sweaty ass his way. Maybe he's the concierge and he was putting the finishing touches on my room. I'm not above lounging in a blue-water paradise called The Humpback.

The closer he gets, however, the clearer it becomes that this man is most certainly not the concierge of this resort or any other—unless there is a secret hot-guy resort somewhere in the peaks of a rugged mountain range where employment is exclusively offered to hulking sex gods who drop women's panties to the floor with a mere puff of breath from their perfectly sculpted lips.

Maybe I'm more exhausted than I realized. Either that or Taylor hired models for her wedding.

He comes to a stop on the bottom step to his pier and casually perches his hands on his hips.

"I think you're in here, honey." He jerks his chin toward the bungalow he just vacated as his eyes travel the length of my body behind his lightly tinted designer sunglasses.

There's no need to glance down to know what he sees, and the knowledge sends a jolt of humiliation through my chest. Post-electrocution hair; flushed, sweaty skin; damp, wrinkled blouse and skirt, and legs that haven't seen the sun in seven months.

Before I can ask God to summon a hurricane for distraction, several questions hit me at once.

Did this guy just call me "honey"? Ew.

If this is my bungalow, what was he doing inside?

And why is he trying to hide a smirk—and doing a crappy job of it—with his eyes trained just below my chin?

My brain decides to answer the last one first as my chin reflexively drops so I can determine if perhaps a tap-dancing crab with a top hat has settled on my collar.

To my horror, I've forgotten that my linen blouse is no longer providing my usual modesty and I'm standing in front of this ridiculously hot stranger with my boobs hanging out of a teeny-tiny white camisole and my extra twenty pounds bulging in sharp relief. My laptop bag hits the sand and I gasp as both hands scramble to cover my chest and torso. I'm fairly certain I dodged a nip-slip, but it's a close call.

This transforms his poorly-hidden smirk into a full-blown smile, and—damn him—it makes his ruggedly handsome face even more spectacular. Who is this guy and where did he magically materialize from? Asgard?

But no relative of Thor would have a scar running across his upper lip and a nose that's obviously been broken a time or two. The rest, though? Absolutely. Not only is he tall, he's powerfully built, something I can tell even through the loose-fitting short-sleeve button-down and knee-length shorts. Ropes of sinew and muscle snake through his developed forearms as he holds his pose and smiles down at me, dark eyebrows raised as if offering a challenge.

"My name is not honey, it's Olivia." I'm proud of the even tone I manage—despite my crouched posture and withered state.

His lips twitch. "I figured." Another jerk of his chin. "Like I said, you're in here."

I glance to the bungalow perched at the end of the pier before returning wary eyes to the Asgardian. "Who are you? The welcoming committee?"

Even through the sunglasses, I can make out the sparkle in his eyes. "No, honey. I'm your date."

Chapter Four

Roman

Damn, the woman's a literal hot mess of temptation in an ill-fitting package. Maybe it's the outline of nipples clearly visible in the barely-there tank top or the sunglasses haphazardly jammed on the top of her head and clearly tangled in her curling hair. Or perhaps it's the shapely ass that bounces right by me as she stalks across the pier and into the bungalow mumbling under her breath while her laptop bag and purse drag along the ground. Whatever it is, I'm intrigued. I glance left and right, seeing no one else from this ridiculous bridal party, or my daughter who promised to stop by, and follow her inside.

Olivia, as she so clearly enunciated, has dropped her bags right here in the doorway by her delivered suitcase as if tugging the load one more inch out of the walkway is simply out of the question. Then again, I've never seen Banks–a self-proclaimed sweat machine–sweat more than this poor woman. She veers left, then right, then trips right over the end of the bed to land face first on the mattress without even a squeak. I consider my options, but Hannah's texts while I flew over here were pretty clear: I'd be sharing a bungalow with my date, and I was to make sure she looked good at all times.

I creep forward, unsure if Olivia's dead or simply so dehydrated she's a husk of a woman lying down before she gathers herself once again like a phoenix rising. A sandal falls off her foot and hits the plexiglass floor below. Tropical fish scatter underwater at the disruption. I gaze down at her, taking in the shapely legs, the delicate ankles, and the heaving back. Ah, so she is alive.

"You okay, honey?" I tap the side of her foot with my hand.

She grunts but otherwise ignores me. I rip the sunglasses off my face and pace the tiny bungalow. It's not much more than an octagonal room with a miniature bathroom attached on one end. The porch with the hammock looks perfect to park my tired body, though. I'm not much for sharing space, but I know what I signed up for. Surely two adults can be civil enough to get through wedding activities. And hey, I can always sleep outside on the hammock if she turns out to be intolerable.

"I'm Roman, by the way. Your date for the week." My voice breaks the silence in the room. Olivia grunts again and I take that as encouragement to keep going. "I hear your ex is kind of a douchebag, is that right?"

Why not get on her good side by slamming the ex-husband? I know how this shit works. I've been around enough of the hockey wives to know how to appeal to a woman's vanity. I have confidence I can make any woman look good on my arm, but first she has to sit up.

With a mighty groan, Olivia rolls over on the bed,

golden brown hair sticking to her forehead and slender neck. Her eyes blink open and before she can speak, my gaze is distracted. Damn, this woman is killing me.

"You're, um...well . . ." I point in the vicinity of her chest, where one of her boobs has slipped the confines of the tank top as if it has better manners than its owner and wanted to say hello. Her light tan nipple is staring right at me. I wiggle my finger in greeting.

Olivia shrieks and bolts upright, tucking herself back into the tank top, much to my dismay. Her breasts are actually quite gorgeous. A handful and a half, and not that fake shit that stays in one place like firmly installed door knockers. Hers look one hundred percent real, which is a pleasant surprise.

"Good god, we need to start over!" Olivia gasps, face turning the kind of red you only see when someone's been out in the tropical sunshine all afternoon without sunscreen. Her sunglasses slip off her head and clatter to the floor to settle with her sandal. She's a pretty mess. A grumpy delight. She's absolutely not the type of woman I usually date, which amuses me to no end.

I'm used to women who look like they stepped out of the pages of a magazine, fully airbrushed and professionally coiffed, so delicate that I fear I'll mess them up just by giving them a practiced air kiss. Hannah was right to ask me for my help for her friend's mother. There's no way I can let this woman go into a long wedding weekend with her ex looking like this.

I clap my hands together, startling her. "Okay, here's what you're going to do, honey. You're going to take a shower and change while I call the spa." I'll get a bevy of stylists in here to work their magic. The full package of hair, makeup, nails, and waxing. And whatever else women do that turns them into show ponies.

Olivia vaults off the bed and stands with her hands on her hips, which thrusts her breasts against that thin tank top I'm beginning to love. She catches me staring and folds her arms across her chest, the glare on her face harsh enough to take off the top layer of my skin better than a derma-planing session.

"I don't know what you were told about this week, but I turned down a date for the wedding. I certainly don't need to share a bungalow with a stranger. And I definitely don't need you telling me what to do. I've got this."

I lift an eyebrow. Women. Of course Holly's mom is one of the stubborn ones. I take a step closer to her, fascinated with the little freckle on the side of her mouth, just like Marilyn Monroe's. On anyone else, I'd bet money on it being fake, but I had a feeling Olivia wouldn't even think to fake a beauty mark. Plus all that sweating would surely have smeared it.

"Taylor, is it?" I ask, referring of course to the bride-to-be we're all here for.

The fire in Olivia's sky blue eyes turns cold. And I hate it. I much prefer the flash of fire that shows up every time I call her honey.

"You seen her yet? Five-foot-five and a size negative two?"

Oliva's eyes narrow but she dips her head in the barest of nods.

"Highlights, perfect brows, Botox since she was old enough to frown? Probably has a trainer five days a week, and hasn't let chocolate pass her lips since puberty. Am I getting this right?"

Olivia huffs in defeat. "She's gorgeous." Then she lifts

her arm and points right in my face. "Don't you disparage her, though. I can dislike my ex without criticizing another woman."

Ah, my date has a strong moral compass. Yet another reason to like this woman. And to think, I had low expectations of even trying to tolerate her. "I didn't say a word. Just hoped to highlight what we're up against here."

"We?" Olivia fires back almost instantly. "I don't even know who you are."

I give her my best smile, but she remains unmoved. "Yes, we. I'm here to make you look good."

Olivia kicks off her one remaining shoe and tries to push a lock of wayward hair behind her ear. "And just what are you getting out of this, Mr....?"

"Roman LaFontaine. Otherwise known as Hannah's dad. At your service." I hold out my hand and she takes it, giving it a rough up and down pump before releasing me. God, she's cute when she's grumpy. I figured she already recognized me, but maybe Olivia isn't a hockey fan. "My daughter is everything to me. She asked me for this favor, so here I am."

Olivia looks at me warily, but I don't miss the way her gaze keeps dropping to my chest. "And that's it? You just jump on a plane and help out a stranger?"

"For my daughter, yes." I point my thumb over my shoulder in the direction of the bathroom. "If you want to take a shower, I really do have appointments with the spa already. That'll give us time to get to know one another and make this believable."

"What do you mean, give us time?"

I grin, wondering how many more frowns I can get out of Olivia before she finally gets in that damn shower and accepts that for just this week, we're a team. "We're getting a couple's spa treatment, honey."

The woman is an awful singer.

After swearing on my daughter's life that I'd remain outside on the hammock while she showered, Olivia hauled her suitcase into the bathroom and disappeared. I took the time to call the spa and double up our appointments. I don't really need a pedicure or another haircut, but I'll get one anyway just to stick close to Olivia and make sure she gets all dolled up. A massage will feel good on my shoulder. It ached the whole flight out here.

"Daddy?"

One eye pops open and I lean over the hammock to see Hannah approaching on the pier with another girl her age.

"Hey, honey." I spring out of the hammock, ignoring the pain in my knee, and pull my daughter in for a hug. Damn, I've missed her.

"This is Holly." Hannah introduces me to her friend and we shake hands. She looks like a younger, miniature version of Olivia. Happier too. Where Olivia is all frowns and suspicion, Holly's bright smiles and enthusiasm.

"Oh my gosh, hi, Mr. LaFontaine!" Holly gushes, letting go of my hand so she can give me a hug instead. "Thank you so much for being my mom's date! She's going to just love you!" Everything she says ends in an exclamation point, so much like Hannah I can't help but like her.

I give her a genuine smile, feeling quite old after being

addressed as Mr. Lafontaine. "Just Roman, please. And it's my pleasure."

Holly giggles and Hannah joins in. The two are dressed in the tiniest string bikini tops I've ever seen. Thankfully they have skirts covering their bottom halves. I open my mouth to ask Hannah if she brought any other swimsuits, but Holly beats me to it, which is just as well. I don't need to start this weekend off with a parental lecture about appropriate square footage of bikini material.

"Mom is probably freaking out about being here, but don't worry, she'll let loose after a glass of wine. Oh! But don't let her have the whole bottle. She sometimes calls Dad names when she's had too much." Holly giggles again.

I glance inside the bungalow, but I don't see Olivia emerge from the bathroom yet. "Anything else I should know about your mom?"

Holly thinks about that for a second. "Her favorite flowers are peonies, her stomach is beyond ticklish, she hates hot coffee these days for some reason, and she's a better dancer than most of my friends. Not that she dances much these days. Oh! And she hates people shortening her name."

A loud curse from inside the bungalow sets the girls off in another fit of giggling. "Thanks for the tips, ladies. If you don't mind, my date and I have an appointment at the spa."

"Good luck, Mr.--I mean, Roman!" Holly says as Hannah grabs her hand and they rush back down the pier.

"Thank you, Daddy!"

Hannah's grateful smile is all I need to gird my loins and go back into the bungalow.

Chapter Five

Olivia

It took the entire length of my blessedly cool shower to allow the reality of my current situation to register, but I'm proud to say my head has not exploded. Yet.

While Roman LaFontaine is clearly unfazed at the prospect of cohabitating with a strange woman in such tight quarters, I don't share his casual indifference. We'll be booking him separate accommodation as soon as I dry off and dress in clothing that won't get me arrested.

I can't help a groan as I wrap the fluffy bath towel around me and secure it. The reality that accidentally flashing my sweaty boob at a stranger is the most action I've gotten in four years is truly pathetic. While it was humiliating, for sure, my embarrassment is luckily tempered by my confidence that this man—Hannah's father, of all people! —has no shortage of naked women thrust at him on the daily. My boob is merely one in a sea of thousands of bobbing mammaries surrounding this guy, so he's likely immune.

He projects so much testosterone, I'm surprised I'm not experiencing a contact high in the form of spontaneous chest hair sprouting beneath my towel. I'd be lying if I said I wasn't a little curious about him. Hannah's never mentioned her dad, and he wasn't there for move-in day or Parents' Weekend at Blue Ridge U, so I assumed he was out of the picture. At least now I know where Hannah got her height and gorgeous smile.

The air in the bathroom is muggy, despite my cool shower, and I pray to all the gods that there's an air conditioner in this joint as I face myself in the mirror for a post-shower evaluation. The red blanketing my skin has thankfully receded, leaving me feeling almost human. And I'm pleased to see I no longer resemble a raccoon in heat with smudged travel makeup. Still, I can't help but replay Roman's comments about Taylor as I stupidly compare her to the reflection before me.

No part of me longs to be that young again—with age comes wisdom, experience, and respect, all commodities worth more than perky breasts—but I can also admit I have no desire to look or feel old enough to be the mother of the bride. Something Hannah's father clearly knows and is determined to prevent for some reason.

His spa plan isn't the worst idea in the world, and it might give me just the fortification I need to face the afternoon. But I'm nobody's charity case, something Holly knows and has somehow let her good intentions allow her to forget. I'll simply explain to Mr. LaFontaine that his time is better spent with Hannah—from the comfort of his *own* room—and that I'll be happy to accept his offer of a date for the wedding day itself, as long as he stops calling me honey and learns my name. Showing up to your ex's wedding with a hot man on your arm is far from a bad move, and Roman is here anyway so why not?

I quickly dress in a stretchy skort and loose tank with a gauzy beach cover-up thrown on top before slipping on my favorite lavender Livvies and hauling my suitcase back out to the room. A small yelp escapes when I momentarily forget that half the floor is plexiglass and I'm not actually about to tumble into the blue water below.

"Is that what you're wearing?" Roman asks from the doorway to the spacious deck, looking like he's just sprung from the loins of Triton and landed on the pier. It's not only his build or his handsome face; it's the confidence with which he carries himself–not to mention the clothes that look like they were tailored just for his body.

I glance down at my outfit before returning my eyes to him. At least he didn't call me honey. "You said we were going to the spa, not the Queen's coronation."

He nods, mouth still turned down at the corners. "It's a good thing I enjoy a challenge."

My chin jerks back at that. "Excuse me?"

Hurrying forward, he drops his sunglasses back on his nose before wrapping his fingers around my upper arm and escorting me out the door without another word. We're halfway to the beach before my steps grind to a halt on the pier.

"I don't have my phone."

"Don't need it." His fingers tighten as he tries pulling me forward.

I don't bother acknowledging his comment, instead yanking my arm free and going to fetch my phone. His foot is tapping on the wooden planks when I return.

"We're gonna be late," he grunts, thankfully allowing me to walk beside him without manhandling me this time.

We only get a few feet farther before I halt again. "I forgot my allergy medicine."

I ignore the tic in his strong jaw and turn for the bungalow again as he shouts behind me, "What are you allergic to? Relaxation?"

When I return this time, he's apparently found his Zen space because he makes no other comments about my behavior, instead falling into step beside me as we reach the sand. Since I've had zero time to explore the resort, I let Roman lead the way, fully planning on hiding behind his giant frame if we happen upon Scott and Taylor.

However, he has different plans—something I discover when he laces the fingers of one of his hands with mine and gives me a gentle tug to his side. I can't remember the last time I held hands with a man.

"You're going to have to at least pretend to tolerate me if this is gonna work, honey."

I can hear the smirk in his voice as a line of hardened calluses brush my palm. The man works with his hands, that much is clear. Based on his muscular build and tanned skin, it's possible he's some kind of tropical GQ lumberjack.

"About that," I begin, scanning our surroundings for familiar faces. The resort is quite small, I'm discovering, and I start to wonder if the wedding party will make up the entire guestbook when I only spot tanned departing couples exiting the lobby.

"About what?" Roman prompts, and I pull my focus back to our joined hands while he opens a door leading into the blessedly cool spa foyer.

"As soon as I've had my massage or whatever, I'm

heading back to the bungalow to get ready for the cocktail thing while you go to the front desk and get a room of your own. I appreciate your willingness, but consider yourself off the hook until the wedding day, Roman."

Instead of arguing with me or even frowning, he squeezes my hand and leads us to the counter where he addresses the attractive attendant, "LaFontaine party for the couple's romance package, please."

It seems I've learned one thing about Roman LaFontaine, at least: the man is deaf.

"Dry skin," the aesthetician tuts as she examines my half-naked body in the same dispassionate manner my elderly dermatologist might. I drop my eyes to ensure my towel hasn't shifted and exposed me to the room—or more precisely, Roman.

The man is lying on his own cushioned treatment table a few feet to my right, enjoying the enthusiastic ministrations of his facialist. "It's always refreshing to treat clients who understand the value of a good exfoliation and moisturizing regimen," she waxes before they share a conspiratorial chuckle. I consider hurling my phone at him. He might not look so dashing with a welt on his forehead.

"It's the change, isn't it?" Gloria, my facialist, asks as she runs her fingers over my cheeks.

"Pardon?"

She waves a dismissive hand. "The same happened to me when I reached this stage in life. Menopause drains your skin of collagen and moisture, so you need to be twice as vigilant."

I bite my cheek to keep from clapping a hand over her mouth. Setting aside for a moment that she's not only right but is attempting to be helpful, I don't need her announcing to my perfect specimen non-date that I'm in the throes of peri-menopause and losing my ever-loving mind!

"Are you having other symptoms? I gained a good thirty pounds over three years." Gloria pats her belly. "Hot flashes? Focus issues? Insomnia?"

"Really, I'm fine," I assure her, although she and Roman appear to share the same selective hearing because she's undeterred. I can only hope Roman is too busy with his skincare fan club to hear Gloria at all.

"I have just the thing—this wonderful local tea that will make you sleep like a drunk grandpa." She smiles, and I muster a brittle one in return.

Dashing my hopes, Roman pipes up from his table. "She gets hot flashes. Lots of them."

Maybe I'll hit *myself* with my phone to end my misery.

"Well, I hope you're being a good husband and giving her control of the thermostat," Gloria offers as she places a hot towel over my face. Oh, good. I'll just suffocate myself instead.

"Her wish is my command," Roman responds, earning him two adoring sighs before he's smothered with his own hot towel. I'm left to enjoy some blissful silence until we're ushered to the couples massage portion of our treatment agenda thirty minutes later.

The masseuses instruct us to disrobe and lie face down on the tables before they close the door, leaving Roman and me alone. In bathrobes and nothing else.

"So, tell me about yourself." Roman looks my way as he effortlessly hops up to sit on one of the massage tables, his legs dangling over the side. I avert my gaze when his robe gapes to expose his chest and a good portion of muscled thigh. Good god. Dampness springs to my skin's surface, and I start fanning myself without thinking.

Roman's lips curl in a knowing smile, and it takes great effort not to roll my eyes. I choose to glare at him instead. "It's warm in here."

It's not technically a lie. The lighting is dimmer in this room, reedy music lilting softly from hidden speakers and a heavenly jasmine scent perfumes the warm air. It's almost romantic, I hate to say. Which I'm sure is the point.

He lets me off the hook. "Okay, so I'm getting the picture you're warm a lot. That's not a whole lot to go on if we're hoping to convince anyone we're in a relationship."

I lean against my own table and cross my arms over my chest. "Why do we need to do that again?" Honestly, this feels like overkill. And I've already decided he'll only be my wedding date, not that he appears to agree.

"I told you Hannah and Holly have their hearts set on it, and I happen to be pretty good at this kind of thing."

"Pretending to date someone?"

"Winning." His grin is twelve kinds of naughty now. "And don't try and tell me your ex invited you here out of the kindness of his heart, because we both know that's bull-shit. He wants to rub your face in his good fortune, and the last thing he's expecting is for you to have an ace up your sleeve."

"Someone's a little full of himself." I reluctantly find myself grinning back. "But it doesn't mean we have to share a room."

"It does if we don't want to be found out by nightfall."

Shoot. He does have a point. What couple vacations together in separate rooms? I chew on my lip as I consider my predicament. I'd been prepared to focus on the kids and let Evie protect me from any Scott blowback, but playing defense is beginning to sound like rolling over. Especially when the opportunity to beat Scott at his own game has fallen in my lap.

Decision made, I draw in a deep breath before exhaling. "Okay. I'm in."

Before Roman can respond, there's a knock on the door. "Ready?"

I turn to see a modesty sheet resting on my table, but I have zero clue how to get under it without Roman seeing more of me than either of us probably wants. Without thinking, I turn back toward him as if he may have the answer, but all words die in my throat when I see he's dropped his robe and is settling his fully naked body on his table, ignoring the sheet entirely as he comes to rest on his chest with a contented sigh.

I'm dumbstruck. No, I'm ass-struck. Because he has the most perfect ass—not to mention back, thighs, and shoulders—I've ever seen outside of a movie or an airbrushed European magazine. Who *is* this guy?

But I can't afford to stand here frozen forever, so I quickly remove my robe and dash under the sheet, pulling it up to cover my butt just as the doorknob turns. I can't bring myself to glance over to see the direction of Roman's gaze.

The vibe remains calm, so much so that I accomplish the impossible and convince my heart to stop its attempt to escape my chest wall. By the time my masseuse tells me to roll over onto my back so she can work on my front, I'm so relaxed, I don't even care that Roman is in the same room.

I drop my head to the side to say something lame like, "I could get used to this," but when I blink my eyes open, I choke on my own saliva instead.

All eyes swing my way, including Roman's, but when he sees the direction of my gaze, his eyes drop down his supine frame as well—where a very impressive erection tents the flimsy sheet now draped across his lap.

Instead of being alarmed or embarrassed, he simply shrugs, his voice gravelly like he just awoke from hibernation. "It happens."

When I realize I'm still staring at his penis, reflex kicks in, and I move to slap a hand over my eyes. But my woozy relaxed limbs mean my aim isn't very accurate, so I end up punching myself in the face instead.

"Wow, honey. I'm starting to worry I might need to call for backup."

<h1 style="text-align:center">Chapter Six</h1>

Roman

"Do you trust me?"

Olivia looks up at me through unnaturally long lashes that the makeup artists glued on after the hairstylist created soft curls in her honey brown hair. The lashes give her doe eyes, which are surprisingly charming on her. "No."

I barely restrain the eye roll and instead grab her where her pretty pink-and-white top is clinging to her pale shoulders. I suggested a spray tan at the spa, but Olivia turned me down flat. Apparently faking a tan on a tropical island is where she draws the line in my extensive glow-up plans. With a quick tug downward, I pull the shoulder caps down to her arms, making the sundress strapless instead.

Oliva yelps, but I hold firm. "Believe me. This way does wonders for your breasts." I shoot her a wink that does exactly what I figure it will: Olivia gapes at me, heat creeping up her neck and into her cheeks. That's nice too, far prettier than the fake rouge the artist added with five different brushes that seemed redundant but who was I to call attention to this perceived error?

"I don't need my breasts spilling out in front of my ex-husband!" Olivia snaps, flailing about, trying to knock my hands off her arms.

I tilt my head, taking in the full length of her, slowly, carefully, catching every detail that had been hidden by her sweat-drenched drab outfit from before. Her skirt hugs her curves, highlighting her feminine landscape in a way that ensures I don't have to fake male appreciation. Olivia Wylder is pretty under all the grumpy bluster.

"You sure about that?" I drawl.

Olivia finally wrenches away from me, but she doesn't pull the cap sleeves back up onto her shoulders and I consider it a victory. I slide my hand into hers, our fingers lacing, before pulling her out of our bungalow and down the pier.

"Come, my sweet Ollie. We have a cocktail hour to crash."

"Wait! I forgot my phone!"

I do roll my eyes then, but dutifully turn around so she can run back inside and grab her phone. The woman would forget her head if it wasn't attached to her body. Then again, something the aesthetician said is echoing in my brain. Menopause. I wince, but quickly school my features when Olivia comes back out the glass door. I take her hand again and we make our way to the resort all lit up by candles and torches along the coastline.

"Okay, so follow my lead and whatever you do, find me adorable."

Olivia snorts not so delicately and it makes me smile. As

the group comes into view, I let go of her hand and put my arm around her waist, tucking her into my side possessively, exactly like I'd do if this were a real date. Olivia sucks in her breath, but she doesn't push me away. If anything, with each step closer to the group, she leans more into my side, which is curious.

"Mom! There you guys are!" Holly gushes, running over with Hannah by her side. A tall man-boy comes over too, looking just slightly older than the girls and not nearly as happy to see us.

Olivia hugs the girls and then the tall kid, before turning to introduce us.

"Roman, this is my son, Dylan. Dylan, this is... Roman." Olivia tucks herself back into my side and for a split second, I forget this is all a farce.

Dylan eyes me warily, but he shakes my hand anyway. I can only assume that Dylan was told about the true nature of this date, but I don't have a moment alone with him to confirm it. A booming male voice has all of us turning. An older version of Dylan is barreling toward us, the blushing bride on his arm. Heads swivel and if this were a teen movie, there would be an audible gasp from the crowd as they sense the drama below the surface as the two exes come together.

"Olivia. You made it." Olivia's ex lets go of Taylor long enough to hug his ex-wife. It's awkward, mostly because I still have my arm around Olivia's waist and there's no way in hell I'm letting go. Not when that asshole has his hands on her. They pull back and I thrust my hand in the space between them.

"Hi, I'm Roman." Olivia's ex eyes me up and down, but shakes my hand, comically squeezing hard, like he has something to prove.

"And I'm Taylor!" The bride pipes up, almost like she knows she's been forgotten by her fiancé but she's determined this wedding will go off without a single hitch.

"Scott Wylder, and this is my bride-to-be. Glad you could make it," he finally says, releasing my hand and tucking Taylor into his side, much like I have Olivia. "I have to admit, I was surprised when a plus-one checked into the hotel. You RSVP'd for just yourself." He says this to Olivia, his face tugging into a bit of a condescending smirk.

I'm expecting Olivia to smack back with something witty and withering like she does with me, but she doesn't. I look down at her and see her cheeks heating and her eyes on her shoes. And suddenly I'm angry. What kind of spineless man needs to flaunt his new marriage in front of his ex-wife?

"We like to keep things private," I finally say, answering for Olivia.

"Well, we're very glad you're both here," Taylor says kindly. Then she redirects her soon-to-be-husband and the two of them move off to talk with some of the other guests.

The kids escort us to a tallboy table and Olivia seems to unlock one muscle at a time as she leans against me. The kids are rattling on about some beach they visited today and the fish they saw underwater. Just when Olivia is finally standing on her own two feet and pulling away from me subtly, three women and one man approach the table, broad smiles all the way around.

The tallest of the group speaks first. "Hi! We're so excited to meet you! I'm Melissa, the oldest of Taylor's sisters. This is Jessa and her husband, Dave. And then the baby of the family until Taylor-the-oops-baby came along, Cassandra." Then she looks at Olivia's kids and announces, "We're your new aunts!"

"Well, I guess we're step-aunts, but that's a mouthful," Cassandra adds sheepishly.

Olivia elbows Dylan and he clears his throat, stepping forward with his hand extended. "Hi, I'm Dylan and this is my sister, Holly."

I shake my head, wondering why their dad didn't introduce his kids to his fiancée's family before the wedding, but that isn't any of my business.

Melissa ignores Dylan's hand and throws her arms around him, pulling him into a hug and then releasing him to inflict her hug on Holly. The other sisters follow suit, all of them looking remarkably like Taylor, just with a few more years added to their appearances. Olivia glances at me quickly, looking uncomfortable. I don't blame her. This is more awkward than the time I walked in on Banks and some puck bunny he was hooking up with in the bathroom of our favorite hometown bar. The woman had literally looked over his shoulder, squealed when she saw me and asked for my autograph while my friend was balls deep inside her.

"Why are you making that face?" Olivia whispers, leaning into me again.

"Funny story I'll tell you about later." I ease her in front of me and skim my hands over her hips, nuzzling into her neck to whisper. "How long do we have to stay with these assholes, you think?"

Olivia pulls back with a sputter of laughter. I slide my hands from her hips to her ass and she freezes. "Work with me, Ollie," I whisper.

Her eyes light with fire and she opens her mouth to blister me, but she's cut off by her ex.

"Wait a minute. You're Roman LaFontaine? From the

Florida Storm Chasers? I knew you looked familiar!" Scott is suddenly by our side, his attention back on me. He's got that look fans get when they think they know you because they watch your games on television.

I paste on the practiced smile and peel my hand off Olivia's ass to bump his outstretched fist. "That's right. Hockey fan?"

Taylor sputters by his side. "No way. I'm the hockey fan. I'm just embarrassed it took me so long to recognize you!" She laughs and then gasps. We all turn in her direction. She's pointing at my date's feet. "Are those Livvies? Oh my god, I love them! It's my dream to own a pair!"

Olivia's gaze snaps up and she looks uncomfortable. Well, more uncomfortable than she did when we first arrived, if that's even possible. "Oh, thanks."

"Olivia has this little hobby of 3D printing in her spare time," Scott explains to the group at large, though no one is looking at him.

Olivia shrugs. "True. Never met a 3D printer I didn't instantly love."

"Mom, your shoes are straight fire. All the sorority girls want them," Holly adds, smiling at her mom.

"Wait. You're *that* Olivia? Olivia, the founder of Livvies?" Taylor's voice is in danger of being in the range only dogs can hear.

Come to think of it, I've seen those sandals before too. One of the hockey wives was wearing a pair and going on and on about them. Olivia made those shoes? That brand? I feel like this information is important enough it should have come up when we were at the spa. She should throw it in her ex's face that she's a business mogul. Forget the hockey player on her arm, she's a major fashion brand.

"Olivia is wildly talented," I say, giving her a pointed look and an eye waggle. *Go on, brag*, I try to communicate through my eyebrows. Olivia looks at me like she's lost.

"They're selling decently," Olivia hedges.

I open my mouth to dispute her modest account of a major fashion brand hitting the celebrity scene, but we're interrupted.

Another woman comes rushing over in heels that are aerating the lawn beneath us. "Oh, there you two are. Dan is looking for you!"

The happy couple walk off again in the direction she points, and Olivia lets out a sigh. The woman reaches out and squeezes Olivia's arm, leaning in to whisper, "I got you, girl. I'll keep them occupied the rest of the night."

Olivia mouths *thank you* and the woman runs off.

I squeeze Olivia's waist and peer down into her flushed face. She seems so feisty with me, but she wilts like a flower in the summer sun when her ex opens his mouth. I don't like it. Don't like it at all. "Ready to blow this popsicle stand before you break out into a sweat?"

Olivia blinks and looks up at me with appreciation shining through her expressive eyes, perhaps for the first time ever when looking in my direction. "Yes, please."

I don't waste any time whisking her back onto the pathway that leads away from the resort the minute her goodbyes to the kids are over. The beach is blissfully quiet and free of people. The sun is sinking into the ocean on the horizon, shadows being cast in the last light of day. Olivia is still letting me hold her hand even without witnesses around.

"You looked all hot and bothered for me back there." I shoot her a wink that works ninety-five percent of the time with women.

Olivia is that five percent. "Get over yourself," she snaps, pulling her hand away from me and marching ahead.

Which is fine by me. Her spunk is back and I get to watch her luscious ass in that dress. Win-win, baby.

Chapter Seven

Olivia

I need some distance, so I'm grateful when Roman doesn't pick up his pace to catch up to me as I head for the Humpback. As if our supposed relationship wasn't implausible enough to begin with, now I find out he's a professional hockey player? This charade was a stupid idea. But at least this news sheds some light on the source of those endless stores of confidence he draws on. It might also explain why he thought he had the green light to grope my butt in front of everyone.

When I slide open the bungalow door expecting to feel chilled air from the air conditioning I cranked up before we left, I'm sorely disappointed. While the humidity has been knocked down a bit, it must still be eighty in here. A bead of sweat trickles down my spine, and I take that as a sign that I should dive into the water a few feet from here and sleep there. I might get eaten by a shark, but at least I'll be comfortable when it happens.

"Chilly in here," Roman comments from behind me as I hear the door close.

I turn and narrow my eyes. "You literally work all day on a giant slab of ice."

He shrugs, dropping his sunglasses to the bedside table and toeing off his shoes. Something about the man in bare feet by the bed infuses the room with an intimacy I'm not ready for. Naturally, my eyes go to the bed. It's a king mattress with a waffled white duvet and piles of fluffy white pillows that are calling my name.

"That's different. I'm working up a sweat on the ice."

The visual his comment conjures is not one that will help my body temperature one bit. I'm such a cliché.

Before I can say or do something I'll regret, Roman continues, "Your ex is a piece of work."

"He's a piece of something alright." I normally don't let myself waste time thinking about Scott, but it's kind of hard to ignore his existence at his own wedding. My purse hits the bed, and I slip off my own shoes. "Honestly, he's not worth talking about. All of that is in the past, and I just like to focus on my kids."

"Makes sense," Roman agrees, stepping toward me. "I can tell he's intimidated, though."

I cough out a laugh, trying to ignore Roman's looming presence as he gets even closer. "Of course he is. You're a professional athlete who could crush him like a bug. Thanks for the heads up on that, by the way." His lips twitch at my sarcasm, and I continue, "Did he do that handshake thing? The one where he squeezes hard until you wince? He did that to my brother and dad at Holly's graduation last year." Piece of work, indeed.

"He tried. But that's not what I was talking about. He's intimidated by *you*." Roman finally halts only a couple feet from me. I can smell his spicy cologne, the same one that had me almost swooning despite myself when he held me close to his firm chest at the party.

"Ha! Scott is not intimidated by me, I can promise you that." While we've both had successful careers, Scott's earnings have always exceeded mine, even with my latest boon. And his ego deserves its own zip code.

"Ollie, guys aren't that complicated."

I interrupt him with a frown. "Why do you keep calling me that? I can't decide if it's worse or better than honey."

He pretends like he didn't hear me. "This business you've got—the one with the shoes—it's a big deal, yeah?"

I automatically shrug. "Sort of." But that's not true, so I straighten and look Roman in the eye. "Yes. It's a big fucking deal."

He throws his head back on a laugh, and I can't stop staring at the thick column of his throat. "Where was that response back at the cocktail thing? You let him walk all over you."

"I don't want to sink to his level—especially not in front of our kids."

"Nothing wrong with standing up for yourself. That's all I'm saying." He goes for the buttons on his shirt—one that undoubtedly cost more than all my shirts combined —and doesn't appear to be planning to stop anytime soon.

"What are you doing?" I fight my instinct to step back.

"Getting changed."

Before I can think, my eyes drop to the smattering of chest hair over his hard pecs. "For what?" I force my gaze back up to his face. *Get a grip, Olivia.*

His eyes sparkle with a combination of amusement and something else I can't quite pin down. "The look on your face right now makes me want to say 'bed,' but I'm going for a run. Gotta get my miles in."

Sweet relief floods my veins. It's time to set some ground rules. "Speaking of, I figure one of us will sleep on top of the covers and the other one under. I call top." No way am I burning up under that duvet with night sweats.

The sparkle turns downright naughty. "Always been a fan of the woman on top."

I shove him aside and disappear into the bathroom where his deep chuckle follows me. The last thing I need is to see Roman LaFontaine naked again.

When I emerge ten minutes later—devoid of the tarantulas that were posing as eyelashes—Roman is gone, but Evie is splayed out on the bed, nose to her phone and a pair of loose pajamas covering her slim frame.

"Oh, thank god," I say into the room.

Evie immediately flips over and grins at me. "Tell me Holly wasn't bullshitting me about this Roman guy being a pro athlete." She's way too excited for my liking.

"No bullshit."

Her grin widens. "I couldn't have planned this any better if I'd done it myself. Those girls are geniuses. This is so perfect."

I shuffle to the bed and collapse on it, landing sideways beside Evie. "I assure you, it's far from perfect. The man is very full of himself. And very attractive." I mumble the last part.

"That's why it's perfect, don't you see? A man like that knows what he's doing—and I mean that in the dirtiest way possible. He's also probably not the kind of guy who gets clingy, which makes him the perfect candidate to end your dry spell."

"Are you comparing my sex life to a drought? Actually,

that's pretty accurate." Let's just say things aren't exactly like a trip to the water park down there these days.

Evie pats my hand. "It's time to get back on that horse, and you know it. What better time than now when you're sharing a room at your ex's wedding with a prize-winning bronco?"

I wrinkle my nose and frown at my friend. "Okay, too many equine metaphors for me. I'm getting Catherine the Great vibes, and it's disturbing. Besides, Roman would never think of me like that."

"His hand on your ass says otherwise." She nudges my shoulder.

"We were pretending." He was doing a better job than me, but I did my best to act familiar around him.

"Was he pretending when he came to your defense tonight? Holly said he stood up for you—repeatedly—when you let Scott be his usual asshat self."

I hate that my kids have to witness all the passive aggression when Scott and I are in the same room. Lying to myself that they don't sense the tension isn't working anymore.

"I'm not going to give the man a verbal beatdown in front of our kids, Evie." Pushing to stand again, I pace to the thermostat. "And not in front of his new wife, either. I have no desire to start a war."

Although, maybe Roman has a point and I should do a better job of standing up for myself. What kind of example am I setting for Holly and Dylan when I play the tolerant punching bag? And why is this thermostat not letting me drop the temperature any further?

"I think Scott did that all on his own when he decided to upend your life to feed his ego," Evie comments from the bed.

I grit my teeth against the memory. It wasn't as if I

was oblivious to the problems in our marriage, but I hadn't expected his midlife crisis to obliterate it. Scott's not a bad person, but he has his issues, the worst of which is his sense of entitlement. I just didn't know he felt entitled to change our entire lives–and my personality–without my consent. The Porsche and the gym membership, I could have handled; deciding on a whim to sell our house and dictate my new role as trophy wife was ten steps too far. I honestly didn't know who he was anymore.

"Which is why I divorced him." I stab at the button again, but nothing happens. "I've moved on, and so has he, obviously." I spread my arms to indicate the very reason we're even in this room right now.

"I thought my teeth were going to break at the cocktail shindig from holding my smile so tight. Did you know Scott reserved the entire resort for the week? And they flew here in a private plane?"

I turn, my brows spiking at Evie while she continues, "Ask me how I know." She rolls her eyes because we both know how Scott loves to brag.

My frustration subsides as I look at my best friend. "Thank you again for looking out for me."

"Always." She reaches a hand out and I step closer to take it. "Now let me continue looking out for you by helping you pick out what to wear to bed to drive Mr. Hockey wild." Her brows wiggle. "Your hair is fabulous, by the way."

I finger my curls, soft and wrestled into submission for once. "It was Roman's doing, if you can believe it."

Evie jerks her hand back. "He's a professional athlete *and* he does hair?! Where did they find this guy?"

My responding laugh is more of a snort. "He didn't do

my hair; he took me to the spa and forced them to beautify me."

If it's possible, her expression turns even brighter. "Even better. He definitely has style. All the more reason to dress in a sexy nightie. Please tell me you brought one."

"Evie, give it a rest. I'm not sleeping with Roman." And the sexiest thing I have for pajamas is an oversized t-shirt printed with the words, "Not all math puns are terrible. Just sum." Not that I'm telling her that.

She directs a pointed look at the bed under her, clearly not ready to give up.

"We're sharing a bed, not bodily fluids."

"You are the only person I know who can make sex with a hot hockey player sound not only clinical but gross."

"What can I say, it's a gift."

Evie's eyes shift to her phone and she laughs. "Uh oh, looks like I've stretched Dan's patience as far as it will go." She turns the phone screen to me and there's a text from her husband.

> Dan: It's an international war crime not to fuck your wife in an overwater bungalow in paradise. Get your ass back here and leave Olivia alone.

Dan and Evie are as hot for each other now as they were twenty years ago, and it makes me happier than I can say that my best friend has that. "You'd better go before he comes over here and hauls you out, caveman style."

Evie climbs off the bed and stands, but before leaving, she wraps me up in a hug. When she pulls back, she tucks a curl behind my ear. "Any man would be lucky to have you, Olivia. No matter if he's a pompous CEO or a hockey player with great taste in asses. You are a prize, my friend."

I squeeze her arms and lean in to kiss her cheek before she flounces to the door and lets herself out. Then I go directly to the phone on the nightstand and call the front desk. "Sorry to disturb you, but what are the chances I could get a portable fan or two for my room?"

Chapter Eight

Roman

I didn't want to interrupt Olivia's conversation with Evie, who I'm guessing is her best friend based on the way she ran interference for Olivia at the cocktail hour. I also didn't want to be seen coming back to the bungalow after a measly thirty minutes of running. My knee was screaming at me before I hit a mile and even my hip was acting up out of nowhere. So suffice it to say, after a quick rinse in the outdoor shower, I slumped onto the hammock and waited the girls out while I lamented all my various injuries. It wasn't a bad place to pout, given the stars up above and the splash of water below. I nearly fall asleep there except for the bugs that start to come out. Before I turn into a walking mosquito bite, I creep inside and slide beneath the covers of the bed.

Olivia is already asleep above the covers like she promised, practically hugging her side of the bed in an attempt to get away from me. I shake my head and smile into the dark at this woman's antics. Then I have to quit smiling because the fans are drying out my mouth and making my lips stick to my teeth. When the hell did fans get added to the room? I hunker down beneath the covers and make it like a tent, sheltering every single part of me from the arctic wind tunnel outside.

I wish I could say I woke up that way, but I'd be lying, and while I'm not opposed to a well-positioned lie here and there, I can't stand by while I start lying to myself. I have standards. Instead, the first rays of sun splash into our room to find me spooning Olivia with the type of morning wood that can't be explained away as anything else. The covers are a thick barrier between us and yet I can still feel the warmth of her curves pressed against me in the most tantalizing way. I should move away before she wakes up, but there's something forbidden about how clearly I can see the back of her neck. The way her chest rises and falls with each inhale and exhale. The soft skin of her ear and the curve of her cheek that is not blushing or sweating yet today.

My hand is on her waistline and I badly want to shift it upward to brush against her breast. I don't, of course, because even I'm not that much of an asshole. But I want to.

I know the instant she's awake because I can feel heat begin to rise off of her like a furnace and every muscle in her body goes rigid. I wait her out while she gets her bearings. Thankfully I'm already braced for the elbow that jams into my gut.

I roll away from her, laughing and groaning in equal measure. "Damn, woman. Good morning to you too."

She huffs disgustedly. "What the hell was that, LaFontaine?"

I pout, something I'm very good at. "I was freezing with

all those fans. I guess I was looking for the closest source of heat. Face it, Wylder. You're one hot mama."

She groans and rolls out of bed to stand and glare at me, her hands on her hips. Her breasts are clearly not roped into a bra–based on the headlights pointed right at me–and I berate myself internally for not going for the grope before she woke up. The T-shirt is funny though.

"You promised to stay under the covers!"

"I am under the covers!" I lift my arms up and point down at myself. Olivia's gaze snags on the tented covers above my groin area and she flushes a delightful shade of red.

She throws her hands up in the air with a huff and spins away for the bathroom. "I'm taking a shower! You...take care of that thing!"

I burst into laughter as she slams the door to the bathroom. I stack my hands behind my head and try to figure out why I find Olivia so fascinating. She clearly doesn't like me, but that doesn't stop me from teasing her. It's just so damn refreshing to be with a woman who isn't falling all over herself to be with me. I know that makes me sound like a douchebag, but it's true. There's never been a drought of women in my life. Not in high school, college, or in the league. I've never had one climb into bed with me and cling to the side like a life raft of chastity.

The shower turns on and I roll out of bed to head for the deck outside. Without allowing time to talk myself out of it, I drop to the deck and crank out fifty pushups as I watch the fish swim below me. When I feel like my chest is screaming, I roll over and match the number with sit-ups. When I feel like I've at least done something to make up for my lackluster run last night, I head back inside the igloo that is our bungalow and pick up the phone to call the front desk. Once they've promised to deliver an extra blanket at some point today, I rest easy that at least I won't freeze tonight.

My phone lets out a few harp notes with an incoming text from my mom. She set her ringtone on my phone years ago. Said I'd know it was her every time I heard notes from heaven. It was her subtle way of not only comparing herself to an angel but also reminding me that she would not be on this green earth forever. Mom is the queen of guilt trips.

> Mom: The Miami Bugle has an article about your team and they have exactly one sentence about you.

I groan. I specifically told my agent to take the week off so I could relax on vacation and not be reminded of my career circling the drain. Leave it to Mom to bring up shit I'd rather forget.

> Me: Does anyone even read the Bugle?

> Mom: I do, jackass, so listen up! Quote: The only thing LaFontaine is adding to the roster is their team quota of retirees.

I rub my chest against the sting.

> Me: Ouch.

> Mom: Reporter is James Smithe. All fancy with that extra fucking 'e'. I say you show up on his doorstep and show him you still got the muscles of a twenty-year-old. Rough him up a bit.

I sit on the bed and try to breathe through the panic

that squeezes my throat whenever I think about the longevity of my career. My mind wants to play for at least another ten years, but my body is screaming out a different tune.

> Me: I can't beat up a reporter, Ma. I can handle some shit-talking.

> Mom: Well I can't! I'm going to have a bag of dicks delivered to his office.

> Me: Jesus. No. Do not do that.

> Me: Mom? Do not even think about it.

> Me: Promise me, Mom.

> Mom: Calm down. Dick-shaped cookies, not real dicks. I'll get a kick out of knowing he's eating a box of dicks. Let me live my life, son.

I shake my head and throw the phone on the nightstand. Mom will do whatever Mom wants to do. She's a ball buster from the era when you didn't have to worry about being sued or smeared online. She raised me by herself and did a damn fine job of it, so I don't call her to stop her evil genius plan. It would be kind of funny knowing the reporter was biting into dick cookies. Clearly, I got my maturity from my mother.

"You okay? Or did the freeze out last night stop blood flow to the brain?" Olivia asks behind me.

I spin around to see her standing in the doorway of the bathroom in a black and white polka-dot swimsuit with a ruffle running diagonal across her torso. With her hair up in a high bun she looks like a pin-up girl. All that's missing are the red lips.

"Hey." My gaze dips before I can wrangle it back upward, cataloging the push of breasts and the flair of hips. And the long, shapely legs ending in pink toenails and matching pink sandals.

Olivia cocks her hip out and settles her fist there. "This must be some fifth dimension of hell where I have to wear a swimsuit in front of my ex-husband and his teeny tiny bride."

I manage to force my eyes upward and lock in on her face. "Pretty sure this is just Belize, not hell. And I don't see what the issue is when you're far prettier than your ex's new bride."

Olivia's eyes go wide and then she scoffs, waving her hand through the air while she goes in search of her belongings. "Oh please. No one's around. You don't need to lie."

I rear my head back. All my teasing yesterday was because Olivia had shown up like a hot mess, but that didn't mean she wasn't flat out gorgeous. She just had to spend the afternoon at the spa and put on a pretty outfit and she could compete against women half her age. I have to rectify this immediately. I'm not sure how, but I have to do something.

I walk over to where she's rifling through her suitcase and put my palms on her luscious ass and give that flesh a healthy squeeze. Olivia stiffens with a gasp.

"So does that mean I can't grab your ass because we're alone? Because I really want to when you wear that swimsuit," I growl into her ear. I don't miss the way she shivers. I give her another squeeze before sliding my hands to her hips and pulling her back into my chest. She'd have to be in a coma to not feel my erection pressing into her. "We may be part of the older crowd at this wedding, but we're still hot."

Olivia melts into me for a moment and time stands still. Hope rises in my chest that she might start trusting me. Then she opens her mouth. "I've never been what you'd classify as hot, Roman. Not now and not when I was twenty and cellulite free."

My mind flashes back to the last thing I heard Evie whisper to Olivia last night. Something about being a prize. Everything clicks into place and anger stirs under my ribcage. My mission at this wedding isn't to put Olivia's ex in his place. Fuck him. Who cares about that guy? My mission is to put Olivia in her rightful place as a queen among women. Aging doesn't make us less valuable, no matter what that asshole reporter implied in The Bugle. And I'm going to prove it to Olivia before this week is up.

Chapter Nine

Olivia

"Remember, you can look all you want, but please don't touch."

"Just like the strip club," Dan mumbles to Roman out the side of his mouth as we all listen to the boat captain's instructions. Evie and I share a look, both shaking our heads.

To say our dates are getting along would be akin to saying chocolate lava cake tastes *okay*. Roman and Dan started chatting sports as soon as we sat down on the boat, and they haven't shut up since. Which is fine with me because it gives me the chance to focus on the ocean view instead of Roman's bare chest and the acres of firm, tanned muscle revealed by his snorkeling uniform of board shorts and flip flops.

Ever since he slid his hands over my body this morning and pressed his hard-on against me, I've been *way* too attuned to his presence. The cracker box size of our room isn't helping, either. When he stepped around me to go take a shower earlier, the brush of his elbow on my arm had my nipples tightening like he'd just bent to get a taste. It's maddening and tantalizing and terrifying all at once.

"I still can't believe the kids ditched us," Evie whispers, affronted on my behalf.

Holly, Hannah, Dylan, and his friend ,who goes only by the name Chugger, were no-shows at the dock earlier, so the boat taking us on our coral reef snorkeling adventure had to leave without them. Which is a shame since I've been here for almost twenty-four hours and have had no alone time with my kiddos. I'll have to pin them down when we get back from snorkeling.

It didn't escape my attention that the entire time we waited on the dock for the boat, Roman's eyes kept wandering to the beach, his frown deepening as each minute ticked by with no sign of the kids. When I asked if he was okay, he shook himself out of it and smiled, telling me it was nothing, but the smile was forced. And his eyes continued to drift to the beach.

I'm guessing his relationship with Hannah is more complicated than I may have assumed. His instant willing-ness to come on this crazy trip at her behest already hinted at a degree of fragility in their connection, but that frown tells me there's a lot more lurking under the surface. Maybe I should ask if he wants to talk about it. Hell, he's going above and beyond to help me; I owe him something. Although the clear joy he gets from pushing my buttons could arguably be payment enough in itself.

"We treat the reef like a museum so others can continue to enjoy it after us," the captain continues, sending a chastising glare our way. I immediately straighten in the vinyl seat, willing my brain to ignore the press of Roman's thigh resting alongside mine. At least I'm wearing a cover-up over my bathing suit in case my nipples start getting ideas again.

The boat rocks gently as the captain continues to instruct us on how to dive underwater to get a closer look and then clear our snorkels without surfacing. When he's sure we've absorbed the appropriate knowledge, we're invited to step into flippers and slip into the clear turquoise water to enjoy the world's second largest coral reef.

If I thought moving would give me relief from Roman's proximity, however, I'm proven dead wrong when he stands and holds a hand out to me. His expression is a nonverbal dare topped with a barely hidden smirk.

"Shall we?" he asks as the dozen or so passengers line up to exit the boat at the back.

"Come on, sweetheart, let's show 'em how it's done!" Scott whips his T-shirt off and tosses it on the row of seats across from us as Taylor laughs and leans into him in her string bikini. I try not to look; I really do. But it's impossible not to check out your ex when you haven't seen his exposed body in over four years.

Whatever fitness commitment keeps Taylor looking toned and trim has clearly kept Scott occupied as well. The flat middle he'd achieved leading up to our divorce has been transformed into a defined, tanned set of abs accompanied by biceps he never even had when we met at Duke as college students.

The urge to keep my cover-up on—even in the water—takes over. How is it fair that the man gets more attractive with age, and I only get fatter, with old hag skin and a foggy brain that makes me feel like I'm approaching dementia some days? God is clearly a man, that's all I know.

Like he's a psychic savant, Roman's jaw tightens as he

glances from me to the happy couple and back again before bending to get his face right in mine. His closeness offers me a fantastic view of his gorgeous golden caramel eyes, the warm irises bordered with a ring of espresso. Yum.

"If you don't strip off that baggy monstrosity, I'm doing it myself. And then I'm throwing it *and you* in the water. You got me?"

I scowl at him, at the same time knowing he's a hundred percent right and I'm being ridiculous. "Bossy much?"

His voice drops lower. "Honey, you haven't even *begun* to see bossy."

His words and their suggestive tone send my thighs quivering so hard I'm not sure I can stand without collapsing in a turned-on puddle on the boat's deck. How in the hell does he do that?

Practice, I remind myself. Lots and lots of practice, I'm certain.

Roman reaches for the hem of my cover-up, so I spring to my feet and start stripping. Thankfully, my thighs recover faster than the rest of me and they manage to hold me up. As I'm pulling the garment over my head, Roman's hands settle on either side of my waist, and I almost fall back into my seat when his scruff brushes the tender skin at the hollow of my throat and his warm lips settle there.

"Relax," he whispers against my skin. "Tits and ass beat skin and bones any day of the week."

Free of the cover-up now, I stare down at the dark waves of Roman's hair as he slides his lips up to my jaw, and an electric current blazes down my spine. My hands move of their own accord to bury my fingers in the thick strands.

"Um," Evie's voice comes from beside me, and when I lift my head, it's to see both Dan and Evie watching us with shit-eating grins. *Dammit*! I grab Roman's hands to pull him off me, but he only entwines our fingers before raising his head and straightening like he's in no hurry at all. When our eyes meet, a fire blazes hot behind his. I'm concerned mine might be a mirror image.

What am I doing? And more to the point, what is Roman doing? Faking a relationship doesn't need to involve all this contact—especially not contact that runs the risk of making me forget this is all a ruse and that Roman LaFontaine is about as interested in getting involved with me as he is in doing his own laundry.

While I'm still gathering my wits, I hear Evie whisper to Dan, "I helped pick out that suit." Oh god. This is so not me. I enjoy flying under the radar and blending with the crowd. I'm not a center-of-attention kind of woman, and I have no desire to be. I like math, I like troubleshooting, I like logic. I don't like being pushed way out of my comfort zone and thrust into the middle of a made-for-TV drama.

"Come on in! The water is great!" Taylor yells, waving from her spot beside Scott in the undulating water below. She's so friendly and energetic, she could almost be a third in Holly and Hannah's little squad. Scott doesn't appear to share her enthusiasm, however, as he frowns up at us.

"After you," Dan says, gesturing for Roman and me to go ahead of them to the ladder.

Once we wrestle our flippers on and descend the ladder, we're enveloped by the cool salt water. It doesn't escape me that the over-sensitized skin at my neck continues to buzz until it's immersed in the ocean.

Evie and Dan join Taylor's sisters a few yards away, leaving Roman and me alone to explore the colorful reef beneath us.

A thought occurs to me, and I'm shocked it didn't hit

me before now. My eyes widen behind my mask as I tread water and turn to Roman, all my senses on high alert. "Do you think there are sharks here?"

His response is a casual shrug as he straightens his face mask. "Probably."

I'm not ashamed to admit a tiny bit of pee might escape at his answer as my treading morphs into more of a thrashing. "Probably? Did my tone suggest any other possible response than 'absolutely, unequivocally not, Olivia'?"

This only makes him grin. "Calm down. I'm just messing with you. The only shark we might see is a nurse shark hanging out at the bottom, and they're harmless unless you step on them. Are you planning on stepping on one?"

I shake my head emphatically, my racing heartbeat still audible in my ears.

"Then we're good." He smiles and moves a swath of wet hair behind my ear. He's being sweet. It's unnerving. "Come on, Ollie, let's go find some fish." That's better. I don't even have the desire to correct him about my name for the millionth time.

We get situated with our snorkels, and I forget about my fears the second we put our heads down and enter the underwater world of twisting coral and dazzling marine life. It's a magical forest of colors and textures with countless species of everything from swaying seagrass to angelfish and black coral. We even see a manta ray skim the sand below us, and I grip Roman's hand in excitement as I point it out. By the time we surface for a quick break, I'm breathless with excitement.

"Did you see that lionfish? It didn't even look real!"

"It's like living in a movie," Roman agrees, treading water beside me.

"I'm pretty sure I saw a great white shark, Olivia!" Scott yells from a few yards over, and I will myself not to react. "Did she tell you she's been self-diagnosed with something she calls Jaws Syndrome?" These words are directed at Roman.

I'd like to imagine Jaws bursting through the water's surface and clamping his teeth around Scott's neck right about now, but I'm afraid it would make me pee again.

I can tell Roman is about to respond, but I beat him to it, yelling, "I should be okay, Scott. I hear great whites prefer their food with less hair." I pat the top of my head, my meaning unmistakable. Scott has always been insecure about his receding hairline.

My comment hits its mark and Scott ducks back into the water with a frown. Roman turns to me and winks before yanking playfully on a lock of my hair and saying, "Come on, killer, let's see if we can find Nemo."

I replace my snorkel between my teeth around a smile and re-enter the fantasy world below with Roman at my side.

Roman

"Hannah just confirmed dinner tonight." I tuck my phone back in my shorts pocket and open the door to the bungalow for Olivia. "I can make a reservation at the resort restaurant for all six of us."

Olivia and I banded together on the boat ride back to shore, texting our kids that we miss them and want to spend time with them. With the night off from wedding festivities, it's the perfect time to see the kids. Honestly, I could go for a night with just Olivia and me, but the lure of seeing my daughter is strong too. I need to spend quality time with her before she flies back to college and refuses to talk to me for months on end.

Olivia plops her bag down on the floor and spins, her huge cover-up whacking me in the knees. Seriously, what is with middle-aged women and these damn cover-ups? Are they supposed to be cute? Because it reminds me of a muumuu. Or the sleeping gowns the women wore in western days. Just wear the damn swimsuit and let us ogle your breasts. Is that too much to ask for?

"Do you mind if we see if they can deliver room service instead?"

I waggled my eyebrows just to see the heat climb up her neck and stain her cheeks. "Damn, Ollie. You want me in bed so badly you can't break for food?"

She rolls her eyes and flips me off, which makes me laugh. "I'd rather not have a reservation at the restaurant. Scott and Taylor will probably have dinner there and I just want our kids to ourselves."

Honestly, I like how that sounds. Our kids. Like I'm part of a team rather than a single dad without a fucking clue, which is what I've been the last nineteen years.

"Sure. I'll have them bring a table, chairs, and enough food to satisfy the wild animals."

Olivia snorts. "You mean you? You eat like a horse."

I rub my flat belly and ignore the ache in my back from that flip dive off the boat I'd done to impress the crowd. "I'm a finely tuned athlete, Wylder."

Now it's Olivia's turn to laugh as she walks toward the bed and pulls the cover-up over her head. I lose the thread of conversation as my gaze zeroes in on her long legs and rounded ass. God, it took all of my self-control not to grab her ass in that swimsuit with the entire wedding party around. I caught Scott staring at her backside once too and almost shoved Olivia under the water to get her out of his line of sight. He had his chance with Olivia and lost it. Not that I have a chance. Not really. But a guy can lust after his fake girlfriend. And besides, Scott thinks we're dating for real. He should keep his eyes on his own woman.

"I'm going to take a shower and get cleaned up for

dinner. Can you handle ordering the food or will it be all low-fat, high protein, and tasteless, Mr. Athlete?"

I prowl over to her, incensed by her insinuation that I eat disgustingly healthy food. I mean, I do, but not on vacation. Her eyes sparkle at me, like she enjoys pushing my buttons. Let's see if she enjoys this. I put my hands on her hips and pull her into my body. She tumbles into my chest, shocked that I'm holding her in the privacy of our bungalow. My hands ache to reach around and find those curves I stared at all day, but I don't want to sport a black eye at the wedding. Instead, I let her feel exactly what she does to me before dipping my head and nipping at her salty neck.

"Are you asking me to join you in the shower instead, honey?" I whisper in her ear.

Olivia lets out a strangled yelp and then she's flailing like a wild animal. I let her go, a cocky grin tugging on my face. She may have felt my erection, but all the flailing in the world doesn't cover up the way her nipples could cut their way out of that swimsuit. I really, really want to grab those straps on her shoulders and peel them down until I free the nipples that clearly want me. I could give them so much attention if Olivia just said the word. All I need is a breathy yes and I'll have her screaming my name in record time.

"You are way too cocky, LaFontaine." Olivia backs away from me, toward the bathroom door.

I adjust my swim trunks, pleased when her gaze follows the motion. "I like it when you talk about my cock." Then I pick up the room phone to order our dinner.

Olivia throws her hands in the air with a frustrated yelp and hightails it to the bathroom, slamming the door in my face and locking it. I laugh as I order dinner and then exit the bungalow. Hopping into the water where it's shallow enough, I grab the side of the wood planks and use them for a pullup bar. When I can't do any more pullups, I do walking lunges up and down the pier. Maybe if I exert enough energy, I can get the erection plaguing me to go down. By the time I have myself under control, Olivia has vacated the bathroom to give me time to take my own shower.

"You look beautiful tonight," I say, pulling out a chair for Olivia on our deck once we're both dressed and ready. The caterers set up our dinner while I was in the shower, our food under gleaming silver domes. The hammock has been pushed onto the pier to make room for our meal.

"Thank you." Olivia tilts her head in thanks and sits, letting me push her in and drape a napkin over her lap. It's the move of a gentleman, but I did it to get another whiff of whatever perfume she's wearing. If the pale pink sundress that highlights the kiss of sun she's gotten the last two days isn't enough to have me off-kilter, the sultry eye makeup she put on will do it.

I sit next to her at the round table, letting my knee settle against hers. She doesn't push me away. Reaching over, I grab the bottle of chilled white wine I ordered and pour her a glass, then one for myself. I hold up my glass and she does the same.

"To a week with our kids," I say before clinking our glasses together.

We each take a sip and Olivia makes a little noise in the back of her throat, like she approves of the wine. "If our kids ever show up."

I check my watch and see they are officially late. "Doesn't stop us from enjoying this wine before they get here." I look out at the picture-perfect view off our deck. "Or this sunset."

Olivia leans back in her chair and sighs. There's a soft

smile on her face that should always be there to take her from beautiful to stunning, but has been suspiciously lacking most of the time I've known her. "I never thought I'd say this, but I'm actually having fun so far this week. I needed a break."

I lean closer to her. "Tell me about it. What did you need a break from?"

My question, or perhaps the alcohol, sets her off. She leans her elbows on the table, cradling her wine in her hands. "This business! I had no idea it would take off like it did. Honestly, if I'd known, I might not have made the damn shoes." She huffs out a mirthless laugh. "Not that I'm not grateful for the success. Believe me. I'm extremely grateful. It's just that a lot of stress piled on my shoulders. I used to be part of a team, and now I'm the one holding the entire bag, and I'm not as good at handling the stress as I used to be. My brain and body sometimes want to fall apart now, like Humpty Dumpty, but there's no king's soldiers to put me back together again. You know what I mean?"

She finally trails off, biting her lip as she turns her head to look at me. And surprisingly, I do know what she means. And I want to unload too. "Um, yeah. I know exactly what you mean. I'm rehabbing at least two nagging injuries at any given time, knowing that every game, when I go out there on the ice, I have to play doubly as hard to be as fast as I was ten years ago. It takes me double the amount of time to recover from a game too. The other guys are out partying and I'm in a goddamn ice bath until I think my nuts might freeze off."

Olivia winces.

"Sorry. Was that an overshare?"

Her laughter sounds like wind chimes in the tropical

breeze. "Maybe, but I get it. And quite frankly, it's nice to know I'm not the only one."

We share a conspiratorial smile. It's when she licks her lips that I realize we're only a few inches away from each other. I can see the way her eyelashes sweep almost all the way up to her eyebrows. The blue of her irises gets a shade darker around the outside ring. Her skin is soft and smooth and shows that she smiles a lot based off the creases around her eyes and the lines from her nose to her mouth. She looks like a beautiful woman who's lived a wonderful first half of her life. I wonder if my face says the same thing.

Olivia clears her throat and we move apart, the moment broken.

"How about we go ahead and eat?" I ask, not wanting our food to be ruined by our late children.

Olivia nods and takes the dome off her plate to see bacon-wrapped scallops, crab cakes, and island coleslaw. "My waistline says no, but my stomach says yes," she murmurs.

"Fuck the waistline. Live a little, Ollie." I take the dome off my plate and dig in. It brings me great pleasure when she does the same.

When we're both stuffed, our plates have been demolished, and the wine is gone, Olivia texts the kids that we're going for a walk and they should come get their food before it goes bad. Holly finally texts back that they're on their way, offering a lame excuse for their tardiness.

"I think those kids have something up their sleeves," Olivia sighs.

I push back my chair and hold out my hand. "They're young adults. I think they always have something up their sleeves. Let's not let it spoil our night."

Olivia puts her hand in mine and even as we walk down

the pier to the sand below, I keep her fingers laced with mine. Miraculously, she doesn't pull away. The sun has set into the ocean, but the resort has tikis illuminating the length of the entire property, giving off just enough light to be romantic.

"I'm supposed to be going for a three-mile run every night to stay in shape."

Olivia gives me the kind of smile that has my blood heating. She squeezes my hand and I can't recall a single time in the last few years where I've enjoyed someone else's company so much.

"Fuck the run. Live a little, LaFontaine."

And with a grin, I do. Instead of working out, I take a long walk on the beach with the prettiest woman on the island.

Chapter Eleven

Olivia

"Another one?" Roman's brows snap together as he catches sight of the new fan housekeeping delivered when they collected our dinner things.

I shrug, surprised at how comfortable I am with this man I just met yesterday. "I get night sweats, and the AC in this room is lackluster at best." When he continues to frown, I roll my eyes. "They brought an extra blanket too—I'm assuming for you?" I toss it to him and he easily nabs it midair.

"Thank god. I don't like having my manliness tested like this. Might need to come up with new ways to keep warm."

I shake my head at his naughty grin and he laughs. He's got a great laugh, deep and rumbly, and it does fabulous things for his face. "You have a great laugh," I share before I can think too hard.

"This time off is giving me reason to use it. Not to mention those kids—Dylan and his buddy were hilarious."

The kids finally showed up for dinner as we returned from our beach stroll. I refused to give much thought to Roman's insistence that we hold hands, even when we were alone, but he thankfully dropped my hand when we spotted the kids outside the bungalow. No need to court questions or create drama where there is none.

"They were showing off for the girls," I inform him as I remove my earrings.

"I was afraid of that." He pinches the bridge of his nose. "How do they grow up so fast?"

"I hate to break it to you, but it wasn't that fast—just like you going from young superstar to Ice Bath King." He glares at me and I smile, snapping the earring box shut. "It creeps up on us one day at a time."

But he's got a point. It felt like not so long ago that Holly had her first crush and Dylan had his first heartbreak, both of them seeking me out for advice or comfort. If this vacation proves anything, it's that my kids have grown into independent young adults who don't need their mom nearly as much anymore. As a parent, it's bittersweet.

Roman shifts the new fan so it only blows on my side of the bed. "Well, I'm not missing any more of it than I have to. I pulled Hannah aside and told her to carve out some time for her dear old dad this week."

"She's a great kid—young woman, I should say."

"Yeah, well, I probably didn't have much to do with that." He's staring at the bed but his mind is clearly somewhere else.

"You don't have to talk about it if you don't want." I make a move for the bathroom to leave him alone with his thoughts, but he halts me with a gentle hand on my arm and a shake of his head.

"No, it's okay. Her mom and I were never a couple, and Hannah has always lived with Angelina while I got to play the 'fun dad' and swoop in to take her on vacation or buy her shit." His eyes lift to meet mine. "The sad thing is I thought I was doing a bang-up job at parenting until Hannah all of a sudden wasn't a little girl anymore. She started expecting things of me that I should have been giving her all along: stability, discipline, priority. Not just stuffed animals and trips to Disney. Let's just say I've been on a steep learning curve these last eight years or so. And I haven't been an honors student." He exhales heavily, and I feel the need to say something to make him feel better, despite the evidence that he might have earned the hard time he's been having with Hannah.

"Well, she clearly loves you." Their mutual affection is obvious when they're together.

Roman musters a smile. "That's because she's a great kid. And I can't afford to mess up anymore. Even a great kid has her limit of patience."

"She called and you flew all the way to Belize to be a stranger's date without hesitation. I'd say that's a good start, LaFontaine."

His eyes roam my face before he says in a low tone, "Let's hope so."

I must be exhausted because my mind reads something into that look and those words when there's nothing there to read. *Stop right there, Olivia.* I force a casual smile. "I think that snorkeling zapped all my energy. I'm going to hit the sack."

"Me too. Gotta get up early to catch up on my workouts." His expression and tone are back to playful. Yup, I was definitely imagining things.

We take turns in the bathroom getting ready for bed, and by the time Roman flips back the covers on his side, I'm snuggled into my pillows with my eyes closed and my nerdy T-shirt covering way more of me than my swimsuit did earlier.

"'Night, Ollie."

I grin despite myself. "'Night, Ice Bath King."

The whir of the three fans fills the bungalow, loud enough to block out most of the insects chirping outside and the water lapping at the pier.

My body is exhausted, but my brain won't allow me to drift off. I remember I have a meeting next week with our new sustainable packaging supplier, and I forgot to ask Ashley to send them my notes. Maybe I should get up and write myself a reminder.

No. I just need to stop thinking. I draw in a deep breath, then let it out, hoping it will take my thoughts with it. It doesn't. I should have taken Gloria up on her offer of that magic sleep tea. I'll have to hunt her down tomorrow.

And now I have to pee again. I slip silently out of bed and make a quick trip to the bathroom before climbing back onto the mattress and settling in again.

After ten minutes, I roll to my back, careful not to disturb Roman. He's nestled under the covers so deep I can't see his head. I have to bite my lips not to laugh. When another ten minutes in this position offers no advantage, I shove a pillow between my knees and settle on my side.

Meditation—that's what I should do. I focus on my breathing, in through the nose, out through the mouth for ten counts. This only succeeds in making my nose tickle. Dammit.

I finally decide to get up and read on the hammock outside before trying again in half an hour like my online research suggested. But Roman's voice stops me.

"What in the hell are you doing over there? Kickboxing?"

I groan. "I can't sleep."

The covers rustle before he replies, "Maybe it would help if you stopped talking to yourself and flailing all over the place."

"I wasn't talking to myself." My neck cranes his way.

"Then how do I know 'meditation is for suckers' and you've only got three chapters left in your book?"

Shit. I was talking to myself.

My feet touch the floor as I shift to sit on the edge of the bed. "Sorry. I'm heading outside to read. Go back to sleep."

"No, you're not." Now he's sitting as well, and I can't help but notice he's not wearing a shirt. No wonder he's so damn cold.

But I wave him off and stand. "It's fine. This happens all the time. I'll get to sleep eventually."

"The mosquitos will eat you up out there." He absently scratches his bare chest and my eyes settle on his firm pecs. "Just stay here and talk to me."

I pause, biting my lip as I try deciphering his expression in the dim room. "Are you sure?"

"Yeah." He pats the bed, and I sink back onto it.

"What do you want to talk about?" This feels weird. It is weird, right? Or is it?

"I don't care. As long as we steer clear of the Bucs' record last season, my daughter's dating life, and any discussion of calendars featuring firemen holding puppies, I'm good."

I snicker at that, relaxing at his familiar tone. "Not a fan of hot firefighters. Got it. How do you feel about Gin Rummy?"

"I should have known you were a ringer when you suggested it," Roman accuses thirty minutes later as I finish wiping the floor with him in our card game.

"Oh, please. It's mostly a game of luck. You're just a sore loser."

"Damn right I am." Is he pouting? "Name one professional athlete who likes to lose."

"Name one who's a bigger baby than you when they do." I shove my cards at him.

He shoots a sly grin my way as he gathers the cards with his long fingers. "It's not my fault I don't have as much practice as those other guys."

My laugh comes out as a giant snort, sending Roman doubling over on his side of the bed. "Good lord. You sound like you're truffle hunting."

I feign offense but do a terrible job when I can't stop giggling. I don't remember the last time I had this much fun with a man. Hell, I can't remember having this much fun with anyone.

Roman grins at me and starts shuffling the deck of cards, but I notice him stifle a yawn.

"Hey." I tap the back of his hand. "I'm sure I can sleep now. It's late."

"You sure?" He's studying me, looking for signs I'm letting him off the hook.

"Yeah." I take the cards and set them on the nightstand before switching off the light on my side. "Thanks for keeping me company, Roman."

He flips his light off, and we both settle on our backs, Roman under the covers again and me on top. "Same."

I smile into the darkness and pull in a deep breath before letting it out and commanding my body to settle. I repeat the actions a dozen times, but it doesn't work.

"Hear me out," Roman says into the darkness, startling me. I was sure he'd drifted off.

"What?"

"I know a surefire way to get your body to relax. It works one hundred percent of the time."

My brows spike. "You've been holding out on me. What's this magic you speak of?"

He answers in the same casual tone you might use while placing a fast food order. "An orgasm."

My mouth opens but nothing comes out. What the...? he can't honestly expect me to rub one out while he lays there next to me, can he?

When I offer no reply, he continues, "I'm more than happy to do that for you, honey. It doesn't have to be a big deal."

He wants to give me an orgasm? Exactly how desperate is he to get a good night's sleep?

"Roman, I don't . . ." I have no idea how to end that sentence. I'm waiting for him to start laughing and yell, "*Psych!*" or something similar.

Instead, he blows my mind. "You know I'm attracted to you, Olivia, and I'm pretty sure the feeling is mutual. We're two single adults with normal, healthy sex drives sharing a room on an island paradise with no obligations other than to have a good time. I can't think of anything that would be a better time than making you come."

Holy. Shit.

Putting aside for a moment that an incredibly hot professional hockey player just admitted to being attracted to *me*—scatterbrained, stressed-out, nerdy engineer, middle-aged me—he's assuming my... situation down there is business as usual. It's definitely not.

Sure, I take care of myself and still have urges—which I can admit have been hitting me with much higher frequency in the last couple days—but I haven't had a man touch me intimately in over four years. *Four years!* That's a lot of time for my body to forget how to do this. How humiliating would it be for Roman to put his hand down my pants and have my body fail to react? I suppose I could fake it, but surely he'd be able to tell, right?

No. I can't do this. Even if it's no big deal to him, no amount of cajoling can convince my mind it's no big deal to me.

"I can hear your brain working from over here. Just shut that shit down and let me touch you."

As if preparing to laugh in my face, my clit spasms at Roman's words. When I feel his fingers brush my bare arm, my entire body trembles.

"Roman . . ." my voice comes out breathy instead of tightly controlled as I intended.

Clearly taking that as encouragement, he scoots closer as his fingers drop to trace circles over my hipbone. Even through my T-shirt, his touch sends sparks between my legs. Without even intending to, I roll toward the center of the bed to give him better access. He doesn't hesitate to tug up the hem of my shirt and slide his hand between my thighs, caressing my skin down to my knee and back.

What am I doing?

Letting Roman LaFontaine feel me up is what!

When he makes his third pass, stopping shy of my underwear each time, I squirm and lift my hips from the bed. He bends his head and places a soft kiss on my belly, just above my c-section scar. I'm too turned on to even think of redirecting his attention away from my flaws. I let out a little moan, and I can feel his lips smile against my skin.

When his hand sweeps up my thigh this time, his pinkie brushes against the gusset of my panties and I almost jump out of my skin.

"Relax," he whispers into my belly. As if he's somehow wrested complete control of my body, I feel myself melting into the mattress as he makes another sweep, this time letting two fingers brush against my now-dampened panties.

Well, at least there'll be no need to fake anything.

The next pass of his fingers elicits a full-body shiver, and he lingers, stroking me through the fabric. My back arches and his lips leave my belly so he can raise his head to watch me. Even in the dim light, I feel the heat in his gaze, and it has me reaching out to touch him.

He pulls back, but his fingers continue their caresses over my hot center. "No. Not tonight. Tonight is about you."

Tonight is about you. Has any man ever said that to me?

I lose all headspace to consider it when he shifts his hand to dip under the elastic and find me wet for him. Skin on skin, his thumb begins a slow swirl on my clit that sends me arching and moaning. Taking this as encouragement, he slides a finger inside for a deep stroke.

"Soaked." His tone is almost a growl, and I spasm around his finger before he withdraws it, only to slide in a second one as he keeps his rhythm on my clit and coaxes me higher.

It doesn't take long before I feel it coming, and I know immediately that it's going to be big. Too big.

"That's right. Take it, Olivia. It's yours," he murmurs from above me, but my eyes are closed. The sensations are too strong, too overwhelming.

Another two pumps of his fingers with that swirling thumb and I'm done. I pant and moan as it rushes through my womb to its peak, and then I'm coming hard around his fingers, thrashing and shouting unintelligible words. "Ah! Oh! H-h-HOCHIMAMA!"

It lasts a long time—longer than I can ever remember any of my self-gifted orgasms doing. When my body finally goes slack, I'm still panting and spasming with aftershocks, a stupid grin settling on my lips. I blink my eyes open to see Roman gazing down on me, a satisfied smile resting on his. God, he's good looking.

"Hochimama?" he asks.

Well, shit.

Chapter Twelve

Roman

Sometimes a man has a right to be cocky, some more than others. When I send a puck sliding between the legs of the opponent who's been chirping in my ear all game, and score the goal, I admit, I'm one cocky son of a bitch. But none of that compares to seeing Olivia come undone under my fingers and then instantly fall asleep like I promised she would.

Her insomnia must have transferred to me because I spent an ungodly amount of time last night just watching her sleep. A little after one in the morning, I came to the conclusion that there's something distinctly different about Olivia. Back in the day, women had tricks up their sleeves like hiding in my bed when I was on the road and staying in hotels with questionable security. Olivia practically pitched a fit that we had to share a bed. I actually had to work to get a simple smile from her. I almost can't believe that she let me between her legs. The trust that she showed by letting me touch her so intimately shifted something in my chest. At the tender age of forty-one, I discover I actually *like* having to work for a woman's affection. The realization kept me up another hour as I grappled with what that meant.

"You going to get up sometime today, Ice Bath King?" Olivia calls from the doorway, looking gorgeous in white linen pants and a bright pink patterned top that highlights her breasts. I blink and look at the clock, stunned that it's already eleven.

"Shit." I sit up and Olivia comes inside. My brain scrambles, realizing I missed my early morning run.

"Evie and I went to breakfast, but there's a group luncheon at noon." Olivia grabs folded clothes out of her suitcase and refolds them. She moves to the bathroom to throw all her toiletries around and then comes back out, hands on her hips as she surveys the room. Probably looking for more aimless shit to do.

I narrow my eyes. She's not looking at me. In fact, she hasn't made eye contact at all yet this morning. That simply won't do. I climb out of bed and grin at the way she's now purposely looking at anything but me. Apparently that hideous picture of a fish above the dresser is fascinating. I walk toward the bathroom, but detour enough to slide my arm around her waist and nuzzle my face into her neck. She gasps and I take it a step further by plucking kisses along her soft skin. There's no explaining away the full body shiver. This woman is hot for me and I'm cocky enough to pat myself on the back in my head.

"Let me get ready and then we can go." I add a healthy slap to her ass, which gets her glaring at me. But hey, at least she's made eye contact.

I don't bother shaving, kind of liking the scruff that's

on my chin and cheeks right now. There's plenty of gray coming in, which is why I usually keep it shaved tighter, but I'm not here to impress any coaches or fans. I can look as old as I want and quite frankly, it's a relief to not be constantly worried about it.

Olivia is swinging on the hammock on the deck when I come out of the shower. She glances at me through the glass door and I slowly put a hand on the knot of my towel. She quickly looks away. I laugh and pull the towel off, selecting a pair of linen shorts and a button up white shirt that will look nice with her outfit. Once dressed, I slide the door open. She's back to ignoring me.

With a hopeful calculation, I make a leap for it and pounce on top of her as the hammock swings wildly at the shift in weight. Olivia hollers, but I hold on tight and wait for everything to settle. When I'm reasonably sure we won't fall out of this thing, I look down at her affronted expression.

"You keep ignoring me and we won't look like an actual couple."

Olivia rolls her eyes, but her cheeks grow a shade or two darker than before. "I'm not ignoring you."

"Oh really?" She's literally looking over my left ear right now. "Then how about you look me in the eye and tell me how much you enjoyed riding my finger last night?"

She hisses and her face absolutely flames. "Roman!"

"Olivia!" I mock. "We're grown adults. I can admit that I really loved your pussy. Can you say the same?"

She glares at me even harder and she's just so damn cute. Her voice drops to a deadpan. "I enjoyed your pussy, Roman."

I shake my head and burst out laughing. Before long, she's joining me and the tension between us has dissipated.

Plucking a quick kiss from her lips, I sit up and attempt to get out of this damn hammock. It takes a couple of tries, and Olivia is still laughing at me, but I finally get to my feet and hold out my hand for her.

She tells me all about her breakfast with Evie as we walk hand in hand to the resort for the wedding party luncheon. It almost feels normal, like she and I have always been filling each other in on how our day has gone. I've never had that before, and this brief time with Olivia has shown me what I've been missing.

We wave and smile awkwardly at Scott and Taylor, who are sitting at the head table out on the lawn that overlooks the ocean. Taylor's sisters and their families are clustered at two other round tables. Shockingly–yeah right–our kids are not here yet, but they have their own table next to ours. Thankfully, Evie and Dan are at our table. I liked him right away on the boat so it's unsurprising that the four of us fall into an easy conversation.

The kids finally arrive, hair wet and sand clinging to their feet. Hannah gives me a quick wave and a smile that warms my heart. Olivia was right, coming here was exactly the right move to start patching things between us. Food is served by waiters in black pants and stiff white shirts, and I can't help but fall in love with all the seafood choices we've had so far. Living in Florida for so long, I've come to appreciate good fish and this place is amazing at preparing it.

"So tell me, Roman, you have brothers who play hockey too?" Dan asks across the table.

I pat the cloth napkin against my mouth before answering. "No. Only child here. Raised by a single mom who didn't know a damn thing about hockey until I started playing. Now she knows more than the game announcers."

"What's your mom's name?" Olivia asks softly.

"Susan. She's a battleax of a woman who I'd want in my corner in a fight." I wink at Olivia. "You'd like her."

Evie makes a noise, but studiously looks down at her plate. Olivia shushes her, which makes me wonder what in the hell those two are communicating about silently. Women are weird that way. They travel in packs and have their own secret language men can't seem to crack. After a breakfast alone together this morning, I can only imagine the things they must have talked about. I secretly hope Olivia bragged about the orgasm I gave her.

"Okay, friends and family!" We all turn in our chairs to see Taylor standing and clasping her hands to her chest. "We have a super fun activity planned!"

Scott also stands, angling toward the kids' table. "But first, you guys are dismissed. Thanks for hanging out at a boring adult luncheon. Go hang at the beach, but wear sunblock!" He has to shout that last part as the kids are already pushing back from the table and running from the resort.

Taylor waits until the last one disappears from view. She literally squeals and I see Olivia grimace in my side view. "We're going to play the Newlywed Game!"

Scott's sisters all cackle with laughter as Taylor jumps up and down at her announcement. Evie snorts behind us and Dan mutters something about needing more beer for this shit. Can't say I disagree with him. Someone from the hotel walks over to Taylor and hands her a box, which must contain all the questions for this insane game.

"Let's have all the couples bring their chairs over here. Everyone has to play." Taylor sweeps her hand to the grassy area without tables. "Cassie? Since you're single, may I volunteer you to be our emcee?"

"Damn," I whistle under my breath, leaning into Olivia. "Sisters are vicious."

Cassandra gives the fakest smile I've ever seen, but comes forward to take the box from Taylor. "All right, everyone. Gather round." Then she mutters loud enough for everyone to hear. "Melissa's single again too, you know."

Melissa gasps but everyone else kind of laughs and follows orders, moving chairs to the center. Olivia tries to grab hers, but I take it, along with mine, putting the chairs right up against each other at the back of the group. If I have to do this shit, I'm going to at least get my fake girl-friend right up against me so I can cop a feel.

Once everyone settles in their chairs, Taylor hands Melissa a stack of tiny dry erase boards that she then distributes to each person with the strict instructions not to share your answer with your partner or you'll be automatically disqualified. Sounds like a good way to get out of this game to me.

Cassandra clears her throat and reaches dramatically into the box. She pulls out a card and holds it up while she reads the question.

"Your husband-slash-partner has the day off. What does he spend the day doing?"

I snort and immediately write my answer, keeping it away from Olivia. Cassandra goes couple to couple and surprisingly, most of their answers don't match. She points at us and Olivia and I flip around our boards at the same time. We lean over to look at each other's answers when the crowd cheers. Both our boards say "work out." I lean over and kiss her to applause.

"Good job, honey."

Olivia winks at me.

"Okay, newlyweds! Let's see your answer!" Cassandra is

pointing at Scott and Taylor. They flip their boards and the crowd groans. Taylor's board says, "shopping for new golf clubs or some other pricey toy." It's a long answer, but it's also wrong because Scott's board says, "getting my bride naked."

Olivia makes a noise in the back of her throat like she's about to throw up. I reach over and squeeze her hand. Safe to say, neither of us is enjoying this game.

Cassandra calls out another question, and Olivia and I get it wrong. Question three and four we get right, which puts us at a higher score than Taylor and Scott. Scott is shooting us glares, so I almost want to get the next one wrong. Poor guy is about to get married for crap's sake and some random guy who isn't even dating his ex-wife is getting more answers right. Clearly, he's a bit lacking in the husband department.

"Okay, folks! Our last question!" Cassandra holds up the card and pauses for dramatic effect. I've gotten stitches on the side of the rink without pain killers that were less painful than this damn game. "What does your wife shout when she has the big O?"

Olivia's horrified stare burns into the side of my head. I hold Scott's gaze as a cocky grin grows on my face.

<h1 style="text-align:center">Chapter Thirteen</h1>

Olivia

I barely suppress the urge to snatch our boards and hurl them into the ocean while pointing in the opposite direction and screaming, "SHARK!" But Cassandra has her damn timer counting down, and everyone is chuckling as they scribble on their boards while hiding their answers from their significant others.

There's zero need for Roman to hide his from me because I know exactly what he's writing as he aims that smug smile at his lap while every ounce of blood in my body fights for purchase in my cheeks.

I glance over to see Scott's gaze lift from his board and hit me before it shifts to Roman and narrows. Oh, for goodness sake. We've been divorced for three years and Roman and I are here for *his wedding*. What reason he has to be in a snit is beyond me.

But I have no doubt Scott remembers exactly what his ex-wife exclaims when she gets hit by a particularly mind-blowing orgasm. It didn't happen often in our years together—as it required a lot of concerted effort on his part—but when it did, Scott would practically hurt himself laughing. To give him credit, though, it never felt like he was laughing *at* me; more like a general euphoria that he could get his wife to speak in tongues once in a blue moon.

Short of faking a heart attack, there's no way out for me, so I release a beleaguered sigh and write the word "Hochimama" with my marker while Cassandra gives a five-second warning. When I feel Roman's eyes on me, his smug amusement is beyond palpable, so I quickly jot one more thing on the board as Cassie gives us the time's up.

"Dan and Evie, you're up first!" Cassandra prompts.

They both flip their boards and high-five when they reveal matching "Fuuuck"s. Everyone laughs.

The other couples are hit or miss, and then it's Scott and Taylor's turn. Taylor flips her board with a huge grin, showing a neatly printed, "Yes, baby, yes!" Her grin drops, however, when she spots the words, "Nothing - she just moans" on Scott's board. Groans all around.

Taking pity on her sister, Cassandra moves things right along. "Okay, Olivia and Roman, you're tied for the win if you get this wrong, and you're the champs if you nail it. What does Olivia shout when you give it to her good?"

I squeeze my eyes shut on a wince as I flip my board, knowing Roman just flipped his own nearly identical one. Absolute silence meets my ears for a good five seconds before every single asshole around us erupts with laughter. Face blazing, I open my eyes again to see Roman leaning forward to read my board where I added a parenthetical to my answer stating, "Not one word from ANY of you about this!"

"We have a winner!" Cassie shouts as laughter mixes

with applause around us.

Before I can react, my hot cheek is caught in Roman's palm, and he turns me to him right before dropping his mouth to touch mine. My surprised inhale has my lips parting, and what I assume was meant to be a chaste lip touch of celebration somehow changes tack when Roman takes advantage and skims the tip of his tongue across my bottom lip. He slides it inside when I let out a quiet whimper.

I can't help it. Something about that man's mouth makes me weak in the knees and weaker in the belly–so much so that I bring a hand up to curve around the side of his neck, digging the pads of my fingers into his flesh when he angles for better access.

Sandalwood mixed with Roman's innate musky male scent fills my nostrils as I draw in a much-needed breath through my nose and shiver at the smooth slide of his tongue and the scratch of his scruff against my skin. The kiss heats when my other hand fists the front of his linen shirt and I swallow his groan as I make my own move to work my tongue against his. He's been in control of the kiss thus far, but my entire body is electric and impatient, so I do what I need to get my message across.

In other words, I attack him.

His hand on my cheek shifts so his fingers spear through my hair to hold me by the back of my head while his other hand skims from my knee to my thigh before settling on as much of my ass as he can reach with us still seated. On his next groan, I'm about ready to straddle him, until I hear more than one throat clearing and a muffled laugh.

Crappity crap crap!

I jump back in my chair, releasing Roman and gasping for air as I glance around at the numerous pairs of eyes pinned on us with varying degrees of amusement. My lips part as I try and fail to remember a single word of the English language.

But it turns out I don't need to utter a thing because Roman says it all when he hollers, "HOCHIMAMA!" to thunderous applause.

"I said it this morning and I'll say it again: I *love* this for you!" Evie squeezes my arm, the surf wetting our bare feet as we stroll the beach.

After lunch and our public make-out session, Roman took off to catch up on his missed workout—but not before dropping another not-so-small kiss on my lips. The entire thing has left me speechless, and I can't make heads or tails of it.

Evie, on the other hand, has already come to her own conclusions—ones she arrived at about a millisecond after I spilled about my Roman-induced orgasm at breakfast this morning. Those being: A) Roman wants to jump my bones, and B) I should absolutely go there.

"I'm glad at least one of us knows how she feels," I grumble.

She splashes me with a swipe of her foot through the saltwater. "It's a no-brainer. Who doesn't want a good old-fashioned holiday fling?"

"*Want* isn't the issue," I admit as I try to sidestep the assault. I mean, I'd have to be an idiot to deny that my body wants this man in every way it can have him. He's awoken something in me that I honestly feared might have been on its deathbed. "Evie, I know it makes me sound lame, but I've never had sex with a man I didn't have feelings for. I honestly don't know if I *can* at this point." Scott and I got married right out of college, and before him, I'd had two steady boyfriends.

"What are you talking about? You totally have feelings for Roman."

She's right; I totally have feelings for Roman. I don't know if it's the vulnerability he showed me when talking about Hannah, or the way he stayed up with me when I couldn't sleep, or his ridiculously addictive sense of humor —or the way my body combusts like a gasoline-soaked torch when he touches me. Whatever it is, I've got it. And I've got it bad.

"Ugh. That almost makes it worse. I don't want to fall for this out-of-my-league hot guy who gives mind-blowing orgasms, only to have him shoot me a casual, 'It's been real' before he disappears in a puff of smoke."

"He's not a wizard; he's a hockey player."

I ignore her comment. "I just don't think I can be a 'What happens in Belize stays in Belize' chick."

Evie halts her steps in the wet sand, so I do too before turning to her.

"Maybe it doesn't have to stay in Belize."

I shield my eyes from the sun, but even with sunglasses, it's a struggle to see her. "Evie—"

Her palm shoots out between us. "You haven't seen how he looks at you."

My head cocks, my tone turning salty, and even I can admit it's self-preservation clawing for control. "And how is that?"

"Like he can't believe his luck."

My protest dies on my tongue. Is she for real?

A choking sound catches our attention, and we both swing our gazes to a walkway leading to the beach, Taylor racing along it, her chest heaving with sobs.

"Shit," Evie echoes my exact thought. "We should go. I'm sure she doesn't want witnesses." She pulls on my arm, but I stay rooted.

"You go," I urge with a nod.

"Olivia, this is not your problem to solve. Of *all* people."

I force a smile as I glance back her way. "It's fine. I'll just be a minute."

Evie stares me down for another few seconds before giving in and retreating down the beach toward the resort.

Taylor falls to the sand on her hands and knees before settling her butt on her calves, her frame still shuddering. She's exchanged her strapless sundress from lunch for a bikini with a silky sarong tied at the waist and beaded flip flops on her feet. There's not a single solitary flaw on the acres of exposed skin.

"Hey." Although my approach is cautious, I still manage to startle her.

She swipes at her tears and tries valiantly for a brave face, but her teeth only lock in a grimace. "Hey." She chokes on a suppressed sob.

Instead of asking the inane question on the tip of my tongue (*are you okay?*), I settle my ass in the sand beside her while I wait for her to gather herself. Only when her breathing evens do I speak. "You guys picked a beautiful place for this week." The truth of my comment can't be denied as we both study the gentle break of the waves on the beach and the lush clusters of tropical palm trees hugging the sand.

"Yeah, I really know how to pick 'em," she mutters, her fingers playing at the hem of her sarong.

Knowing how carefully I need to tread, I consider my words for long moments before sharing, "When Dylan was six, he whacked his head on the cement while wrestling with his best friend."

I feel Taylor's eyes turn to me, but I keep mine aimed at the water—not because I'm ignoring her, but because my own complicated feelings about Scott have risen to the surface with my memories.

"Twelve stitches and a concussion," I continue. "I'm not sure who was more of a wreck, Dylan or me." Before Taylor can ask me why in the hell I'm laying this on her, I get to the point. "Scott was in Chicago at a meeting his firm had worked six months to score, and the minute he got my call, he was in a cab to the airport."

Taylor releases a shaky sigh beside me.

"What I'm trying to say, Taylor, is that Scott can be thoughtless–like anybody–but when it comes to the important stuff, he'll never let you down."

I can hear her thick swallow. "If that's true, then why did you divorce him?"

That isn't really hers to have unless Scott shares his version, but I realize I'm not bothered that she asked me. Unexpected, but true.

"We met when we were practically kids." Taylor can take that however she wants to—it's not lost on either of us that she's significantly younger than Scott. "We both changed over the years, which means our expectations and goals changed too." I shrug. "I won't get into the nitty gritty, but our priorities no longer made us compatible." Not to mention our fights, the growing resentment, and the fact that we were clearly no longer in love. "Even with that, though, we both managed to agree that the kids would always be the one priority we shared."

"I'm worried he doesn't know me at all. How can you make someone you don't even know a priority?"

"What made you two decide on a wedding in Belize?" I ask, finally looking her way. Scott can't resist expensive, ostentatious gestures, but I also know he's not a huge fan of the beach.

"It was a surprise." Taylor's lips tip up a little at the corners while she studies the sand beneath us. "I told him on our first date that it had been my dream vacation ever since I was in high school and saw pictures of thatched huts suspended over blue water. He'd already booked the resort when he proposed."

We exchange small smiles that are not altogether awkward. And it seems my work here is done.

After another minute passes, I push to my feet and wipe the sand from my pants. "Well, I've got to find Evie and then get a little work done. You good?"

Taylor nods and looks up at me from the sand, her glamorous blond tresses reflecting the sun. "I'm not sure how you can be thinking about work with a hockey god camped out next to you." I can't help my grin at the thought, even as my belly dips and my nerves resume their jittering. "Especially with the way that man looks at you," Taylor finishes on a grin, making my eyes widen.

It seems perhaps Taylor wasn't the only one in need of some reassurance. Now I just need to figure out what in the heck to do with this surprising information about one Roman LaFontaine and his apparently obvious regard for a certain hot-flashing engineering nerd from North Carolina.

Who would have ever thought?

Chapter Fourteen

Roman

For the first time in forever, I had miles of energy to burn off, which turned into literal miles of running along the sand. By the time I make it back to our bungalow a sweaty mess and no less attracted to Olivia than when I started my run, Olivia is showered and dressed, standing by the full-length mirror to put on dangling earrings that match her turquoise dress. Far too much of her luscious skin is covered by the material, in my opinion.

"Damn, I missed our shower."

Oliva whirls around and arches one eyebrow. *Damn. Even that's sexy.*

"*Our* shower?"

I swipe a bead of sweat off my chest and watch the way her gaze drops to my torso and has a hard time coming back to my face. "Figured I could get a head start on getting you nice and relaxed for a good night's sleep again. A fingering a day keeps the doctor away."

Olivia snorts and whirls back to the mirror, smoothing her hands down the dress and cocking her head to the side. "I don't know about this dress."

I come up behind her, careful not to get my sweat on her, but unable to stay away either. I dip my head over her shoulder and inhale her scent while looking at her in the mirror. "You make that dress look amazing."

And it's the truth. It's not the prettiest dress. The puffy sleeves are giving me Laura Ashley eighties vibes. And I only know that because Mom went through a phase when I was a kid. All my photos from my youth show her in hideous floral dresses with puffy sleeves. Olivia's isn't floral, and the sleeves are made of some sort of see-through material, but with a body like Olivia's and the tan that she's rocking, she should be showing off more skin.

Her soft smile in the mirror is exactly what I was going for, though. Having gotten a feel for her ex-husband this trip, I know for a fact he didn't give her the compliments a woman needs. A woman can be a badass CEO or a stay-at-home mom, but she needs to know that the man in her life finds her hotter than hell. Not that I'm the man in Olivia's life, but I'm beginning to suspect I want to be. Hence the miles of running today. I have a lot to think through.

"Do you trust me?" I ask in a low voice.

Olivia doesn't hesitate before nodding. I reach up and grab both sleeves. With a quick yank, I rip them off the dress and let them flutter to the floor. Thankfully, they tear cleanly, just a few loose threads left in their wake. Olivia gasps, her jaw dropping as she stares in the mirror. I hold my breath. Then her head tilts again and her mouth snaps shut.

"Well, crap. That does look better."

I shoot her a wink in the mirror. "Of course it does. You

have amazing shoulders and breasts to die for. Why not make them the highlight, not the dress?"

Olivia whirls around and reaches up with both hands to grip my hair and pull my head down. Her lips are on mine and suddenly I'm not in control of a kiss for once. Her tongue dips into my mouth and I'm so stunned I barely participate. I'm just reaching for her hips to deepen the kiss, deepen the connection, deepen everything with her, when she releases my hair and steps back, smoothing her hands down her dress again.

"Gotta go, Ice Bath King. Don't be late to the bachelor party." And without another glance in my direction, she's gone, leaving me with the scent of her perfume in the air.

I groan, dropping my head to look down at the erection that's already back. Not even a ten-mile run could get it to go away completely. "It's going to have to be a cold shower," I tell the room.

Dan, being the upstanding man he is, swings by our bungalow fifteen minutes later to pick me up before we head out to the bachelor party one property away. My knee is acting up on the walk over there, reminding me that I'm not twenty any longer and ten miles was probably overdoing it. Dan tells me all about his kids and asks me questions about Hannah. It's nice to talk about something other than hockey, to be honest.

I love hockey, don't get me wrong. It's been my career for so long it's become my whole life. Everything has been pushed aside for the sport, and while it's paid handsomely for the life I have, it's also left me feeling like I made a few wrong turns somewhere along the way. I should have been more involved with Hannah. And I should have made more time for friends outside of work, like Dan. People who like me, not because I'm some famous hockey player, but because I have other things to offer. I'm not even sure what those other things are, but I'd like to find out. And that scares me too. Because if I want to explore what else I am in this world, that means hockey has to be in my rearview mirror. And I'm not sure I'm ready for that.

We hear the party before we see it. Shouts and loud music assault our ears before we make a turn and see the patio area of the resort next door. Scott has rented out a ballroom and patio area, both of which have been outfitted to look like the inside of a sports bar. Scott is seated at the bar, a Carolina Smokies hat on his head. They're a shit baseball team, but I've always rooted for them too. Can't help but love the underdog.

"Hey, LaFontaine! Come on over here!" Scott has a cigar clamped in his teeth, but he waves us over like we're besties. Dan lets out a sigh, but pastes on a smile as we walk over. "Come meet the guys I met in the lobby." Scott gestures to some younger guys at the bar who are probably just happy to have an open bar and a semi-drunk host.

The new guys know who I am, thanks to Scott's name dropping, but after they snap a few selfies with me, they settle down and we shoot the shit while we sip beers. Scott is alternating beer and whiskey shots which seems like a dangerous combo if he wants to be able to function tomorrow, but who am I to rope him in at his own bachelor party? Scott's on his third shot when he turns to me with a smile that I've seen enough to know to brace myself. Guys always fawn over famous athletes...and then they turn on them.

"I lost a bundle last year when y'all didn't take the cup a second time."

And there it is. The accusation about losing a bet or being disappointed by us not winning the Stanley Cup, as if

I should apologize to the fan. Believe me, I was disappointed as hell too. Jobs are gained and lost because of championship games. I know all too well that not sealing the deal last year made my position even more precarious. You lose, and the owners start looking at who to blame. Being the oldest guy on the team is not a good place to be when the owners and the fans are disappointed in a loss.

"We'll get it this year," I say confidently, looking around for someone else to talk to. Dan got pulled away by one of the other groomsmen a few minutes ago.

Scott grabs my shoulder, that cheesy smile magnified, the one that says we're pals when we both know we are very much not. "I don't know, man. You only have the one Stanley Cup, right? Isn't forty-something pushing the envelope a bit for a repeat?"

Normally I'd smile and walk away. Avoid the drama at all costs. But this fucker is acting like his shit don't stink when I know he's the stinkiest of them all. Which is why I give him a smile back, the one that says open your fucking mouth again and you'll regret it. "And how many Stanley Cups do you have, Scott?"

The new guys all start to hoot and holler and crowd around us, sensing a tense situation and having had enough alcohol not to have the good sense to back away. Scott puffs up his chest, which would have been a better move if I wasn't packing at least twenty pounds of muscle more than him. I butt right up against his chest. He fucking destroyed Olivia's self-confidence so he could feel better about himself. Someone needs to bring him down a peg or two and I'd be mighty pleased to be the one to do it.

A shrill whistle cuts into the tension. All heads spin to the door leading into the ballroom, except for Scott and me.

"The strippers are here!" someone shouts.

Scott breaks our staredown and darts away, shouting something about having dibs. I roll my eyes and release my breath. What a fucking clown. Feather boas and handcuffs are twirling around. The lights dim, but some weird strobe light starts flashing, and it's all giving me a headache. Scott is pushed into a chair and both girls are dancing for him while waiters come by with trays of shots. I turn my back on it all, just wanting to head back to my bungalow.

And Olivia. I want to get back to Olivia, to hear her talk about the bachelorette party or some YouTube channel she recently found all about new resins to be used in 3D printing. Or to play cards with her sitting on the floor. Or spar with her about something ridiculous. Or to get my hands on her sweet body again. To watch her shudder and shake. To hear her heavy breathing when I touch her. Fuck all this shit. I just want Olivia.

I'm almost off the patio when something louder than the music catches my attention. It's Taylor's voice and it's coming from the cell phone Scott is holding up in the air.

It's my bachelorette party and I have all my best friends with me! Check this out! Sissies say hi! Hey! Hi! Okay, now let's go to my newest bestie, Olivia! Olivia, don't be shy. Say hi and tell us all about that hottie you're shacking up with!

Squeals of feminine laughter make my stomach squirm, but I edge back to the party, wanting to catch sight of Olivia. Even if it's from a tiny cell phone screen. She looks gorgeous, of course, her cheeks pink and her eyes bright. Her hair is slightly mussed, but she looks happy.

He's hot, right? Like five alarm fire hot. Have you seen the man's abs? I mean, every woman dreams of dating a hot hockey player. What's not to like? The body, the money, the face, and the...the growly fierceness, you know?

Taylor starts giggling and then it's her face filling the

screen. *Oh we know, Olivia. That man is the complete package, you lucky girl. Now who's going to do another round of shots with me??*

The video cuts out with Taylor blowing a kiss to the screen, probably for Scott, but the whole thing has made me nauseous. Is that how Olivia sees me? Just some famous athlete package that she ogles over? I'm over here running ten miles because my head's messed up thinking she could be someone I'd sacrifice hockey for and she's over there with idea that I'm nothing more than a well put together piece of meat.

I spin on my heel and walk away from the resort without a goodbye or a destination in mind. I end up walking farther north than our resort, the moon reflecting on the water to light my path, before I turn back around and head for the bungalow. My mind is still racing, but my aching joints have officially declared the day over. I need sleep more than I need to figure out why Olivia's opinion of me matters more than anything's mattered in a long time.

Chapter Fifteen

Olivia

"Good god," I mumble to myself in the bathroom mirror. Not only has my makeup melted with my latest hot flash, but my entire scalp is pricked with sweat, making the time I spent on my hair earlier a complete waste. I wet a few paper towels under the cold tap and shove them under my armpits. Ahhh. That's better.

The bathroom door swings open, dance music from the bachelorette party spilling inside along with Taylor's sisters Jessa and Melissa. I nab the towels from my pits and paste on a smile, although I do genuinely like these women from the short time I've spent with them. I'm just not in a party mood anymore.

"Olivia! Hey!" Jessa greets me before ducking into a stall.

"Hey there," I return to them both as Melissa smiles and approaches the mirror a few feet down from me.

"Holy hell!" she exclaims as she gets a look at herself, prompting me to glance over.

"What's wrong?" I see nothing alarming, just a very pretty woman around my age, a shiny blond mane cascading over her shoulders and clear hazel eyes reflected in the mirror.

"I look like a damn raccoon." She reaches for a paper towel and wets it before swiping under her eyes.

I can't help my grin. "At least I'm not the only one." I decide Melissa won't be one to judge, so I repeat my paper towel routine under my arms and get back to fixing my own makeup.

"Genius!" She eyes my impromptu air-conditioning system, smiling at me as she continues leaning into the mirror.

"Goddammit!" We both turn to the stall where Jessa disappeared moments ago.

"Did you fall in?" Melissa asks on a grin.

"I wish. Got my damn period," she groans.

Melissa frowns. "You want me to break it to Dave about the vacation sex for you?"

"Ha! With the way my body's been messing with me, he wasn't expecting any, believe me."

Melissa and I lock eyes, both of us knowing exactly what that means.

"I thought it was just me," Melissa says, turning her attention back to dabbing at her face with the towel.

"We're a year apart, bitch. Did you think I'd let you go through menopause alone? Although, now I've got to start counting my cycles again, so you might be ahead of me."

"I might not be right on track, but I definitely feel both of you," I volunteer. "These hot flashes and the brain fog are killing me."

"Ha! Wait till you start losing your hair," Melissa crows. When I glance at her lustrous head of hair in question, she laughs. Then she shocks me by reaching up to dig her fingers into her hair before lifting off a hairpiece that comprises almost half of her mane. "Oh my god, that feels soooo much better."

"Did you just take off Flossy?" Jessa asks from the stall, sending me back to my bewildered state.

"Yes, and you were right," Melissa responds to her sister before enlightening me. "Every hairpiece needs a name. This one is Flossy because she's so extra." She grins and rolls up the hair, casually stuffing it into her purse before withdrawing a small hairbrush.

She swipes at her hair a few times to arrange it neatly in a less full but still attractive sweep that brushes her shoulders.

I can't help my smile. "It looks beautiful both ways."

She meets my eyes in the mirror again. "I meant to tell you earlier; I love your dress."

I can feel the pink hit my cheeks at the memory of Roman ripping the sleeves off like some metrosexual Neanderthal before I jumped him. Again! "Thanks."

"Any chance that hockey hottie of yours has a single teammate who prefers his women a little more mature?" Melissa winks and moves on to touch up her lipstick.

I groan internally as I replay that stupid display I made for Taylor's Instagram or whatever it was. I didn't realize until after she posted it that it wasn't just a private wedding video, so I'm kicking myself. Sure, it wasn't hard to get me fired up about how hot I find the man, but the other stuff? She wouldn't stop going on and on about all the clichés about dating a professional athlete—like it was something to aspire to or cross off one's bucket list.

I still felt bad about her state on the beach earlier, so when she latched onto me upon my arrival at the party, I let her drag me around while she got tipsy and mooned over Roman and me. Little does she know there really is no Roman and me, but that was the entire goal from the start. Who was I to disabuse her of that fantasy?

Still, I shouldn't have played into it on video like that. I shouldn't have talked about Roman on a video at all. What if he sees it? I'll be mortified at how I sounded, parroting Taylor's mooning. Can you erase an Instagram post? I should have asked Ashley. I should know more about social media in general! I'm a freaking CEO of a fashion brand, for god's sake—no matter how ridiculous that still sounds in my own head.

I realize Melissa is still waiting for a response, if only a joking one. "Considering you're gorgeous and funny, I'm guessing there would be more than a few who'd be all over you." I'm not lying, either. From what I've learned, she's probably a couple years older than me, but her looks and personality would grab anyone's attention. "But unless you're willing to relocate to Tampa, I'd look elsewhere."

"Damn," she says in mock disappointment. "But thanks for the compliment, new best friend."

"Hey, new best friend or sister since birth, is one of you going to get me a tampon or am I going to sit in here all night?!" Jessa shouts from the stall, making us both laugh.

I ditch my paper towels and snag my purse.

Then I help a girl out, glad to be part of the sisterhood.

When I get back to the bungalow an hour later, I'm surprised to see Roman already asleep on his side of the bed. Although the long workout from earlier would have done me in way before now, so I suppose it makes sense.

I can admit my body started dreaming up some scenarios on my walk back to The Humpback, but it's probably just as well I won't get to live any of them out.

Not only because my sense of self-preservation wants to dig a moat around my heart, but because my conversation with Melissa brought something important to the forefront of my mind—regardless of my body's oblivious skip down the Candyland boulevard to hot sex and orgasms.

Roman lives in Tampa, Florida. I live in Charlotte, North Carolina. Last I checked, those two states had two very big states in between. His career is in Tampa—along with what I imagine is a lot of traveling. Mine is in North Carolina. I employ fifty people. I have a large studio and a bustling office.

Which means I have to be okay with anything that happens between Roman and me staying right here in Belize. I need to find the "What happens in Belize stays in Belize" woman within. Either that or put a stop to all of it now before it goes too far.

Put a stop to the flirty looks, the shivers from his touch, the warmth that spreads through my chest when he calls me beautiful. And the trembling in my womb every time I take in his broad shoulders, the thrill from running my fingers through his thick hair, the urge to drop my eyes to his happy trail whenever he's shirtless, the flip of my belly when he calls me Ollie, even though I'd hate it from anyone else.

All of it.

I smile when I notice another blanket has been delivered and is now draped over Roman's sleeping figure atop the first one. And I have to bite my cheek to keep from laughing when I see a fourth fan has also been added, all of them pointing to my side of the bed and set on high.

Though I have no clue what to do about my current Roman conundrum, it's clear I have a good eight hours to puzzle it out. So I tiptoe to the bathroom to get ready for bed and then settle myself under the fans' breeze, hoping I'll be able to sleep without help from my fake boyfriend-slash-potential holiday hookup.

The first thing I notice upon waking is that I'm alone in bed. The second is that the sliding doors are wide open and Roman is snoozing on the hammock outside. A smile comes unbidden to my lips, and I crawl out of bed to approach him.

Somewhere between my tenth and eleventh position change last night, I came to the conclusion that you only live once and I'd be stupid not to take advantage of the clear attraction between Roman and me. It would be one thing if it was attraction despite a personal connection, but he and I click in a way apart from the physical that will make this a special memory to hold—bittersweet, perhaps, but worth it.

"Morning, you," I murmur as I plod on my bare feet across the wood planks. When he doesn't respond, I assume he's sleeping, so I tiptoe closer. His eyes are trained on the rippling turquoise water beyond, so I repeat myself, thinking he didn't hear me the first time. "Good morning."

His only response is a grunt.

Okay. Not a morning person. Good to know.

"Have you had breakfast?" I try again.

Another grunt.

Fabulous.

"Is that caveman for yes or no?" I tease.

This gets his attention, but when he turns his gaze to me, his golden eyes are cold. It's such an unfamiliar look, it literally sends me back on a foot.

"It's dumb jock for leave me alone."

All I can do is blink.

"Roman . . ." I begin but have no idea what to follow it up with.

He fills in the blanks. "You know, it's not like I'm not used to it, but I really thought you were different, Olivia."

Why does it hurt that he called me Olivia instead of Ollie? Still, his tone has my back up. "I'm afraid you're going to have to explain since I have no idea what you're talking about." My hands hit my hips.

He scoffs, his eyes scraping down my frame with contempt, making me wish to god I was wearing more than this stupid T-shirt. "Come off it. You know exactly what I'm talking about." When I give my brows a sardonic raise, he continues to enlighten me. "Bang a professional hockey player on your vacation so you can go back to your snooty-ass friends and brag about how you played the dumbass piece of meat into thinking he had an actual shot."

My jaw drops and my arms fall limply to my sides as my mind races to catch up.

But he's not done, even as he hauls himself out of the hammock to stand towering above me. "The thing that gets me the most is that I knew you were too good for me this whole time. Now I'm starting to understand you're just like the rest of them. Have an awesome breakfast," he bites out. Then he turns to stalk past the doors and down the pier to the beach.

All I can do is stare after him while I replay his words in my head.

"Dammit!" I shout to the ocean when I realize what's

happened. He obviously saw that asinine video and me being a complete asshole playing Taylor's game. I *knew* I should have paid more attention to my assistant's prodding about my social media lameness.

I gather my hair into a bun with restless fingers as I frantically search for a fix to this mess. Of course Roman is offended; I essentially talked about him like some object to be won instead of a sweet, funny, thoughtful, and—yes—hot man to value and appreciate.

But it's even worse than I feared because the look on his face and the words he used told me that I wasn't just some casual holiday hookup to him. He actually cared about not just what I thought of him, but he cared about *me*. And now he thinks I'm some puck bunny who only wants him for his fame.

It's time to set things straight and let Roman know what I *really* think about him before it's too late.

Chapter Sixteen

Roman

My hamstring is fucking killing me and I badly want to kick the pier to let out some aggression, but I have a feeling I'd probably break something and just add to my growing list of injuries. I walked off in a huff without a shirt and now the gaggle of women going to brunch at the resort next door in their island sarongs are eye-fucking me so hard I feel naked and afraid. I'm just pissed off. And if I really dig deep, I'm not even angry. I'm just hurt. And that's an even fucking worse feeling.

My phone rings and I look down at it like I forgot I'm still clutching it in my hand. I pulled up the airline website out on that hammock in the early morning hours, thinking I'd leave the island ASAP. I had no plans to keep helping out a woman who had zero regard for me. Then images of Hannah waking up to her father ditching her flooded my brain and I abandoned that idea.

"Hey, Mom."

"Did I catch you during your workout?" Her scratchy voice brings me a wave of relief I didn't realize I needed.

"Nah. I'm just out for a quick recovery walk."

She makes a phlegmy noise. "Getting soft, are you?"

I shake my head and manage a small grin as I look up at the rising sun. "Nah. Did ten miles yesterday and need to chill today. Are you calling because some other jackass reporter is about to get a delivery of dick cookies?"

"I decided giving away free sugar was not the punishment I had in mind. Enough about dicks, son. I have a serious question."

"Fire away."

"I want to get together for a family reunion."

I pause, thinking she'll explain further. When she doesn't, I tread carefully with my line of questioning. "We don't have any family. It'd just be you, me, and Hannah."

"Exactly. We may be small in numbers but we gotta stick together. Let's do it up here in North Carolina. Say, Charlotte?"

I flop down on the sand and watch the waves lap lazily onto the sand. "Charlotte? That's oddly specific and out of left field."

Mom starts talking so fast I know she's up to something. "Well, you know, Charlotte is a beautiful town. It's close to Hannah's college, but also far enough away we won't embarrass her. And people there might not know you."

It suddenly all clicks. "Did you speak to Hannah recently?"

"Guh, no! Absolutely not. Anyway, I've gotta go book a hotel. How's late June for you? Good? Okay. Gotta go!"

And then the nutjob hangs up on me. I drop my head back and pray for patience. Mom talked to Hannah, who decided to play matchmaker. That's the only explanation for this sudden family reunion in the very town where Olivia resides. What's curious is why my mother is somehow now on the matchmaking train. She's always warned me to stay away from the puck bunnies. Her exact advice was *go ahead and play with them, but don't marry one and lose half your net worth*. She punched me right in the gut when I told her I'd gotten one pregnant. She obviously came to love Hannah and eventually was happy I'd been careless, but her warning still stood. So why is she suddenly going against her long-standing advice and pushing me toward Olivia?

"Roman!"

I pull my head back and open my eyes. Olivia's running down the beach toward me, looking like a homeless version of a Baywatch chick. She has the bouncing boobs and the free-flowing hair, but she's also wearing her sleep shirt and a pair of shorts that have seen better days. The T-shirt's half tucked in on one side and I'm fairly certain the shorts are inside out. She stops at my side, kicking sand all over me before bending at the waist and putting her hands on her knees and breathing hard.

"Olivia?" I'm not happy with her, but I also don't want her having a heart attack out here on the beach the day before her ex's wedding.

She holds up one finger and continues to heave air into her lungs. I reach up and tug her down to sit next to me. Fine strands of hair are sticking to her neck and forehead, but eventually her breathing slows enough for her to talk.

"Thank god you didn't go ten miles again today. I might not have made it."

I can't help the tug on my lips. "Don't run much?"

Olivia rolls her eyes and darts a glance at me. Our knees

are touching and I can't help but want more of her touch, despite how mad I am. "Only if a bear is chasing me, and I purposely don't put myself in situations where that would happen. But I had to find you."

I narrow my eyes, ready for some lame excuse for her behavior that'll be flimsier than the dresses most of the puck bunnies wear. "Why's that?"

She nudges my knee, turning to finally look me in the eye. "I'm sorry about the video. Taylor was drinking and going on and on about you, and said she wanted to document her whole wedding just for herself. I figured since we're here under the guise of dating I should go along with that narrative. Not for one second did I consider that she might post that publicly."

"So what you said was completely fake?" I briefly considered that when I couldn't sleep this morning. Still didn't bring me peace.

Olivia's eyes go softer than the hand she puts on my knee as she turns further into me. "Roman. Of course it was fake. I don't give a crap about your occupation or your celebrity status. In fact, I prefer to stay out of the limelight. What I do care about is the guy who stayed up with me when I couldn't sleep. The guy who loves his daughter so much he agreed to be a fake date at a destination wedding. The guy who has better fashion sense than me and isn't afraid to sleep with four fans blowing on him."

I give up the fight with my lips and let myself smile. "It is kind of like trying to sleep through a hurricane."

Olivia bursts out laughing. Then she rubs my sore knee like she knows I'm in constant pain. "I'm sorry. For the ridiculous fans, the sleeplessness, the hot flashes, and most of all, for hurting your feelings with that video."

All the insecurities and hurt feelings go away in an

instant. I believe her. In fact, I should have believed that the video was her acting right from the get-go. Olivia doesn't talk like that. And if my own insecurities weren't horribly triggered, I would have seen that.

I reach over and pull a lock of hair away from her sweaty forehead and tuck it behind her ear. "So what else do you like about me?"

Olivia's eyes sparkle. She knows I'm just fishing for compliments now, but she gives it to me anyway. "I like this." Her hands leave my leg and cup my face, fingernails dragging through the scruff that's grown out this week. "I like the salt and pepper. It's sexy as hell."

Fuck, I like this woman. "I have a confession."

"Yeah?" Olivia shifts closer and I have to clench my hands into fists to keep from hauling her onto my lap and claiming her lips.

"I dye my hair to keep the grays away." What the fuck is wrong with me? I've never told anyone that for fear of my secret getting out.

Olivia lets out a whimper and then she attacks, throwing herself across my lap and kissing the hell out of me. Our tongues meet and teeth clash, the kiss spinning entirely out of control. We fall back onto the sand and make out like teenagers who can't control their raging hormones. I vaguely hear a whistle somewhere down the beach, but I don't give a fuck. All I care about is this woman and the fact that she's not the puck bunny I feared she was.

My hand slides under the back of her T-shirt and I let out a groan against her lips. The woman isn't wearing a bra. "Shit, Ollie. We gotta slow down or I'll strip you naked right here on the beach in broad daylight."

Olivia jerks her head up and even though her eyes are hazy, she darts them left and right before coming back to me. "I'm going to say something completely out of character for me."

I grin, thumb sliding back and forth on her silky skin. "I can't wait to hear it."

She licks her lips and I groan, lifting my hips enough to grind my erection against her stomach. She inhales sharply but doesn't pull away. "Let's go back to The Humpback."

Every muscle in my body tightens in anticipation. "For?"

Her cheeks go red and I want to shout in triumph. "Seems like we should continue this . . ." she waves back and forth between us, ". . . in private."

I don't wait for her to take another breath. Or to have a chance to second guess what she's offering. I stand, pulling her with me and then throwing her up and over my shoulder. She grunts as her stomach hits my shoulder, but I've already taken off in a dead run toward the pier that leads to our bungalow.

"Roman!" she sputters from upside down. Her hands grab my ass, probably to keep from flopping around as I jostle her, but the feel of her hands squeezing my backside makes me almost seize up and drop her.

"Hands off, woman! I'm getting us to the bungalow!"

"I'll hurt you!" she shouts back, both of us oblivious to the stares from people around us just trying to enjoy an early morning beach stroll.

"I'm not that old, Ollie. I can handle a fireman's carry." Although my knee does send out a dire warning when I have to step up onto the pier. I ignore it.

Olivia finally accepts her fate and lays still, letting me get us to our bungalow in peace. The air conditioning hits us full force as I slide the glass door open. I march right over to the bed and the stack of blankets that are still there.

"Don't you dare–"

I flip Olivia and she bounces on the bed, eyes wide as she stares up at me. I pounce, crawling up on the bed with her, laying my body on top of hers and getting right back to that kiss she gave me on the sand. Speaking of sand, there's some on the bed now, but not even that can stop me from finally getting this woman naked. Olivia sighs into the kiss and slides her fingers into my hair. She tugs hard and it lights a fire in my chest. Fuck, I want this woman more than I've ever wanted a woman before. My hand slides up under her shirt. Her soft belly tenses but then my palm reaches the promised land. Boobs. And Olivia has the nicest set I've ever had the pleasure of fondling.

I rip my mouth away from hers and push up, watching my tan hand cup her exposed breast. Her light tan nipple puckers against the sweep of my thumb and I can't help but drop my head and latch onto the bud. Olivia whimpers, her fingers tightening so hard I feel fire erupt across my scalp.

"Naked," I whisper against her skin. "I need you naked. Right fucking now."

Olivia nods her head. Reluctantly, I rip my mouth away from her nipple and pull her T-shirt over her head. My hands are in the waistband of her inside-out shorts for a split second before I pull them down her legs. They tangle around her ankles, but I can't bother with that right now. Not when Olivia is finally naked and under me, shifting restlessly against the bed. She's gorgeous, all creamy skin with light tan lines, long legs with curves at her hips. There's a c-section scar low on her belly and stretch marks above her hips on both sides. It's like her body is a walking, talking, breathing story of a life. One I want to know every detail of.

"Fuck, Ollie." My voice is unrecognizable, even to myself.

"Don't look too hard," she mutters, breathing hard, but also moving to cover herself.

I grab her hands and hold them above her head. My erection nestles between her legs. I'm back to being insanely angry. No ten-mile run will work here. I need to fuck the low self-esteem right out of this woman. I flex my hips and watch her eyes flutter closed as I hit her in just the right spot.

"Does it feel like I don't like what I see?" I growl. "Look at me."

Olivia's eyes open and she boldly holds my gaze.

"That's better, honey. I want you watching me while I enjoy this body of yours. I want you to see what you do to me."

She nods, looking like she's not quite sure how to take me. And that's fine. By the time I'm done with her this morning, she'll understand exactly how hot she is, even if I nearly die from holding back my own orgasm.

"Keep those hands over your head before you pull my hair out."

Olivia bites her bottom lip and nods again. I shift downward and plant myself between her legs, shoving her thighs apart to accommodate my shoulders.

"I have to taste you." I look up at her one last time, giving her a chance to say no. Once I taste her there won't be any holding back. When she nods, I dive in, spreading her apart for my feasting and licking up her center. Her taste blooms on my tongue and I'm a goner. I growl, attacking her like a wild man, nipping and licking while Olivia cries out my name and nearly bucks me off the damn bed. Her legs begin to quake and I know she's close. I slide one finger inside and hook it, giving her just enough to have her coming undone.

"Ahhh! Hochimama!"

I grin, still flicking that swollen bud that made her explode. My erection is practically drilling a hole in the mattress, but I tell it to wait. Patience comes easier with age, and I've got forty-one years of honed patience. When Olivia finally peels her thighs away from my ears, I kiss her dripping flesh one more time before removing my finger and kissing my way up her stomach and back to those gorgeous full breasts.

"I need two more Hochimamas before we head to the shower and get cleaned up. Can you do that for me, Ollie?" I look up at her, proud of the bloom in her cheeks and the tangled mess of hair against the pillow. She blinks her eyes open.

"I might die if I have two more," she heaves.

I grab the waistband of my shorts, waiting until her gaze drops and she licks her lips. I shove them down, letting my erection spring free. She swallows hard and I can't help the cocky grin.

"But what a way to go, am I right?"

Chapter Seventeen

Olivia

I'm having an out-of-body experience; that's the only way to describe it. Because the Olivia I know wouldn't be openly ogling a beautiful man's penis trying to calculate how many different ways she can have it.

Roman's unabashed enjoyment of my body has me feeling sexier and more empowered than I've ever been in the bedroom—even when I was in my twenties with a tight ass and breasts that laughed at gravity. Everything about him is magic, from his nimble fingers to his talented tongue to the playful teasing and those hot whiskey eyes that drag oh-so-slowly over my skin. I feel like Cleopatra to his adoring Antony, without all the pesky war and double suicide stuff, of course.

Without a clear plan in mind, I shift to my hands and knees and crawl to the end of the bed, never taking my eyes off Roman's proud member jutting from the neat thatch of dark hair. He's ever so helpful, moving closer to the bed until I can easily reach a hand out to wrap my fingers around the base. His groan is my instant reward, but I'm confident I can do better than that.

My tongue rasps over him from root to tip as I stroke the silky-smooth skin covering the shaft of hard, pulsing heat. I swirl my tongue over the head a few times and then spend a long moment at the spot just below that has Roman's body shaking and his breath coming in pants.

"I can feel you smiling on my dick."

His comment has me laughing because he's not wrong. I'm having the time of my life exploring and tasting, seeing which movements and rhythms drive him crazy and making note to use them to my advantage. I get a little carried away after sucking him into my mouth, my hand twisting as it slides up the base to caress the part I can't fit in.

"Slow down, honey. Fuck, your mouth is incredible," Roman grunts, defying his own command with an involuntary thrust past my lips. Then he takes a step back, causing his cock to pull from my mouth with a pop.

When Roman grimaces around a laugh, I realize I let out a disappointed mewl at the loss of him. I was totally getting off on making him so worked up.

But my disappointment is more than assuaged when I catch the intent in his eyes a split second before he flattens me to my back and covers me with his naked body.

Good lord baby Jesus and all the baby disciples.

The weight of his body on mine and the top-to-toe contact is *everything*. I'd sigh and take a minute to fully appreciate it if I wasn't so tremendously turned on. Roman takes my mouth, any signs of gentleness and patience a memory as he plunders like a conquering army of hot dudes invading a tiny village of sex-starved middle-aged nerds.

Our hands glide, fingers pull and scrape, limbs tangle,

breaths mingle and pant until Roman produces a condom out of thin air (I told you he was magic!) and rolls it on. Then, instead of simply sliding home, he rears up to his knees, yanking me closer so he can hike my ass partway up his thighs before spreading my legs as wide as they'll go.

Only then does he nudge my entrance, his gaze riveted to our connection as my clit aches and I beg him for anything he's willing to give me.

"Roman, please." My voice is a foreign whimper, and I can feel the bead of sweat dripping from my temple as I shake my head side to side.

And, though his eyes don't move, he must hear me because his hips jerk back and then he plunges into me in one long, hard, delicious stroke.

"Fuck," he groans, meeting my own unintelligible, "Omiglordy, omi... gaaaah."

When he withdraws almost all the way again, my hips lift to chase his cock, so he uses both hands to hold my thighs apart and keep them right where he wants them. Then he thrusts again, filling me and sending bursts of fire through my womb and up my spine.

"I can't believe how tight and wet you are." Roman grits his teeth as he continues to power in and out, eyes raising from our connection to roam over my breasts and up to my face. I'll probably have bruises on my thighs from his tight grip, but I'll wear them with nothing but satisfaction. "I love watching you take me, Olivia."

Sweat beads on his forehead, a few drops streaming from his hairline and down to his neck. I want to lick them from his skin and then flip him to his back and ride him. But he's nowhere near being done with me.

One hand shifts from my thigh until his thumb finds my clit and swirls. My back arches, and the combination of his cock and thumb send me over the edge in a surprise orgasm. Roman drops to his hands and swallows my cries as his mouth covers mine again.

I circle his shoulders to caress the mountains and valleys of his back as I come down, but he's still driving into me relentlessly, so there's barely a moment to recover before he's working me up again.

In the end, Roman succeeds in giving me all of the promised orgasms as well as enjoying one of his own. But it's debatable which one of us enjoys his climax more. The way he roars and pistons and loses all control before collapsing on top of me brings an almost maniacal grin to my face and pure elation to my heart.

My fingers skim over his damp back, causing a full body shiver that makes me laugh. Since when was sex so freaking fun? I don't remember so much smiling. Clearly, I've been doing it wrong all these years—or maybe I just don't remember since it's been so long.

Roman pulls up to his elbows and aims a drowsy, devastatingly sexy smile at me. Nope, it's not my memory; it's Roman.

"I think it's *you* who nearly killed *me*." His breathing is even more labored than mine.

I choke out a laugh and hold his jaw in a tender grip before lifting my head to kiss him. "Funny, that doesn't sound like a complaint."

"Oh, believe me," he replies, tucking a strand of damp hair behind my ear, "all of my remaining brain cells are busy strategizing how to repeat the last half hour as many times as possible before we have to hit the airport this weekend. Let's take this to the shower and get a head start." His grin is decidedly naughty.

I refuse to let mention of the airport dim my mood,

instead informing him with a grin of my own, "I'm a bit of a math whiz, so I'm happy to help. Just saying."

"Considering my calculator isn't waterproof and I enjoy naked strategizing, that's convenient." He secures the condom before pulling out and launching to his feet with a surge of energy that defies his recent exhaustion.

When he reaches his hand out to me, I happily take it and let him pull me with him to the bathroom.

"I'm not sure I've ever had breakfast in bed before." Roman pops a grape in his mouth before reaching over to feed me one. We've decimated the meal room service delivered after our shower and are picking at the remains of the fruit plate while we laze around in bed. He's not even giving me a hard time about the flock of fans that cooled our eggs and toast before we could enjoy our first bite, so I know he's in the same Zen zone as I am.

"It would take way too much energy to ambulate anywhere after that shower." I bat a strand of hair from my face as the fans ruffle my mane.

I'm in another of my loose T-shirts watching Roman casually draped on the mattress in nothing but boxer shorts and a smile. He doesn't even try to hide his smugness. It's way too adorable and has me thinking I could so easily get used to this.

But that's not what this is.

To that point, it's time to have a conversation we probably should have had before I jumped him on the beach. I straighten and pull the sheet over my legs. Roman reaches over and yanks it back off just as quickly, making me snicker.

"Hey, eyes up here, Ice Bath King," I scold with zero force behind it. He obeys nonetheless. "I just want to make sure we're on the same page about...whatever this is." I flap my hand back and forth between us.

He straightens as well now, face turning serious. "I figured you knew," he begins, making my nerves jangle. But before I can interject, he continues, "See, when a woman attacks a man, he gets an uncontrollable urge to fuck her . . ." My mouth pops open and he feigns deep contemplation before continuing, "Strike that. When an incredibly *sexy, funny, smart* woman attacks—"

I cut him off with a lunge and a shove to his shoulder.

"Case in point!" He easily takes me to my back in a flash and hovers over me, laughing and giving me a memory to tuck away for later when we're no longer in each other's lives.

"You're ridiculous." I smile up at him. He really is gorgeous, the laugh lines around his eyes and mouth making him even more so. I skim my thumb over the scar that cuts across his upper lip and wonder how he got it.

His laughter subsides and he runs the backs of his fingers along my jaw before getting real with me. "I live in Florida; you live in North Carolina. We both have careers, and neither one of us is stupid."

I nod, relieved that we're of like minds. But that doesn't mean there's not a part of my heart that wants to grab onto a belief in the impossible. It's the same part that still thinks there's a slight possibility that maybe, perhaps, there could be at least *one* unicorn living on this planet somewhere and we just haven't found her yet.

"Vacation fun, and no hard feelings." I verbalize it in case he needs confirmation.

"*Naked* vacation fun," he reiterates with another grin.

I thread my fingers through his thick hair, imagining what it would look like if he stopped dying it and ignoring the bereft feeling that comes with the knowledge I'll never get to find out. "Then you'd better get to ravishing me because you've got lunch with Hannah in a couple hours and I've got an inbox full of emails to answer before my office files a missing person's report."

Roman doesn't delay in demonstrating his dedication to our carefully devised shower plan. It's no wonder he's an MVP.

Chapter Eighteen

Roman

"Hannah!" I wave from the table I reserved right on the water's edge at the resort restaurant. I stand and hug my daughter when she gets there. She looks so grown up it scares me. She sits down and smiles at me over the table, the little girl with dimples still in there somewhere. She's just buried under a woman's body and a layer of sophisticated makeup.

"How are things with you and Olivia?" She wags her eyebrows and I try for my best poker face.

"Just fine. For a fake date, I can't complain." I lean over the table and put my hand on hers. I do not kiss and tell. Time to redirect. "What's this I hear about you and Grandma Susan planning a reunion?"

Hannah drops her gaze to her empty place setting before lifting her head and spearing me with the doe eyes that did me in when she was little. They sparkle with unshed tears and my heart dips. I'd pretty much do anything to bring back her smile.

"I dated a guy last year."

My heart is no longer dipping, it's surging in rage. "What? Who? What's his name?" Another thought occurs and I'm halfway out of my chair before thundering, "What did he do to you?"

"Shh! Dad! Sit down!" Hannah yanks on my arm, making me sit before glancing around the restaurant like what total strangers think is more important than some weaseldick hurting my baby girl. "Jeez. I didn't tell you about him because I knew you'd freak. Like you are right now." She lifts an eyebrow, but I won't apologize. Men are douchebags. I play hockey with them. I hear what they say in the locker rooms about girls. Hell, I've said a thing or two in my past I'm not proud of either. That was before I had a teen daughter who started making heads turn. I saw life through a new perspective real damn fast.

I force air through my lungs and try as hard as I can to keep my voice steady. "You're broken up now though?"

Hannah nods. "Yeah. The thing is, Dad, I really liked him." The tears are back and I make a mental note to quiz Olivia's daughter about the situation until I get a full name out of her. "When we broke up, he said something to me that pissed me off at first."

Oh, that little shithead is dead.

"He said I have daddy issues I need to work through." Hannah picks up her water glass and laughs. Actually laughs. I'm over here plotting murder and she's laughing. She takes a sip and shrugs. "Turns out he's right."

I do a double take. "Wait, what?"

She spreads her hands wide. "It's true. I do have daddy issues. You were barely around, and while Mom didn't talk shit about you, she didn't have anything nice to say either. It's fair to say my outlook on men is colored by your example."

I'm floored. The worst kind of guilt and sense of failure hit me full force. "Hannah," I breathe, unable to say anything else.

Hannah grabs my hands now. "I didn't say that to make you feel bad. I know you have a demanding job and Mom didn't make it easy for you to see me when you were available. I just know that I'm an adult now and I can make my own choices. And I want to see you. I want to get to know you."

I squeeze her hands back like they're a lifeline. "I want that too, pumpkin." Everything I've been thinking about with my career comes to a head. And instead of feeling like my life might be over if I no longer have hockey, I get a sense that my life might just be beginning. "I'm probably going to retire. This year or next."

Hannah gasps.

I hurry to complete my thoughts. "I haven't said anything to anyone, but I want you to know my intentions. I was wrestling with feeling like a failure as an athlete. My body's failing me, and I can't deny it anymore." I lift my head and lock eyes with her. "But it's failing you that hurts worse."

"Daddy," Hannah whispers.

"No, I'm serious, kiddo. I failed you as a father your first nineteen years. But if you'll let me, I'll be there for at least the next nineteen."

Hannah's smile is everything. "I'd like that."

I return to The Humpback two hours later, heart fuller than it's ever been. Hannah and I chatted so much about everything my voice is hoarse. Without a lot of input from me, Hannah has become a truly remarkable young woman. For the first time I feel like she and I are headed on the right path. No matter what happens with the end of my hockey career, things are going to be different with us. And that's a vow I intend to keep.

"Hey, how'd lunch go?" Olivia asks, stepping into a pair of wedge shoes.

I blink, brain scrambling for why she's all dressed up again. "Wait, what's today's activity?"

Olivia turns from the mirror, looking amazing in a pale pink sundress. Her hair is in soft waves around her face and she hasn't sweated off her makeup yet. "Rehearsal."

"Ah." I spin in a circle, looking for the appropriate clothes. When I find them, I strip down to my boxers to get changed. "Are we late? I can be ready in five minutes."

When Olivia doesn't answer, I look up, catching her staring at me with her teeth caught on her bottom lip.

"See something you like, Ollie?" Of course she does. I do more pushups, sit-ups, and running than any normal human should do. I wonder if I'll keep up the insane routine once I retire.

She startles, cheeks turning pink. "We're not late. I'm just ready early. Had to take a break from working."

I frown, finally noticing the open laptop and the file

folders strewn all over the coffee table. "Did something happen?"

Olivia sighs and flops onto the loveseat. "Do you know anything about my company?"

I shrug, stepping into gray slacks and fastening them. "From what I've gathered, it's maybe the fastest growing fashion shoe brand since Crocs, and let's be honest, that wasn't exactly fashion."

Olivia snorts. "Agreed. But I don't know that I'd go that far. Livvies is too custom and niche to get that big."

I go to sit by her, thinking the rest of my outfit can wait. Olivia seems stressed and I don't like that look on her. I far prefer that dreamy, unfocused haze that comes over her after she orgasms.

"Still, it's pretty impressive what you've built."

"You know I didn't even intend to make a product and sell it." She shakes her head. "I was just an engineer working at an injection molding company, trying to reduce waste by switching to 3D printed products." She shoots me a grin and I like it better than her previous expression. "My nerd brain got carried away with the technology and I started printing custom-fit shoes for my assistant and me."

"Maybe you should look into hockey skates next. Blisters are no joke."

She snorts. "I'll have to talk to my assistant, Ashley, about that. In fact, if she hadn't taken to Instagram from day one and shared Livvies with her gazillion followers, I'd still be trying to convince the guys at TK Injection Molding to move into the twenty-first century."

"Instead, you're selling the most coveted shoes in the country to Hollywood celebrities." I stroke her bare knee, and she waves my comment away like the multi-million-dollar company she started from nothing was just a day's work. "I am seriously impressed, Olivia," I insist.

"Thanks." She puts her hand over mine. "Don't get me wrong, I am proud of it. But I pride myself more on keeping sight of producing work that's of the utmost quality. I don't want my name attached to anything that's not the best."

"But?" I prompt, nudging her.

She throws her hands in the air, bursting with irritation. "But I can't think! I can't remember my own damn name some days! It's like someone threw a stink bomb in my brain and I'm left wafting away the clouds to try to function like a normal human being. Don't ever go through menopause. You'll regret it."

I'm pretty sure laughing wouldn't be appropriate right now, but she's adorable when she's flailing her arms like that. "I'll make sure to tell my doctor menopause isn't for me."

"Smartass," she grouses, smacking my arm. I do laugh then, especially when she shoots me a dirty look.

"Seriously, honey. Why don't you get checked out by a doctor? The hot flashes, the sleepless nights, the brain fog. That doesn't sound right."

"Don't forget the weight gain and the impending hair loss," Olivia adds before rolling her eyes. "But I've gone to a doctor and he said my only option was hormonal birth control. Which I'm already on!"

I rear my head back. "That's his only solution to a laundry list of symptoms?"

"Trust me, I know. The frustration is real," Olivia grumbles.

I put my arm around her and tuck her into my side. "I

think you need to find a new doctor. I can ask around if you want. I'll get you set up with the best in the business."

She pats my stomach and melts in my arms. "Thanks, Ice Bath King."

"Anytime, Ollie. I know what it's like to grow old and not be able to do anything about it."

Olivia lifts her head, drilling a finger into my abs. "This body is what you call old?"

I feign hurt feelings. "Hey, I have the abs, but you should see the hours I spend in rehab. They don't call me the ice bath king for nothing."

Olivia grows serious. "I know. It sucks when you know you should be able to do something you've always done and then your body just fails you. Makes you start to doubt yourself."

I nod. "Exactly. I see these younger guys doing things I used to be able to do too. Makes me wonder if I have a place on the team at all. Makes me seriously consider retiring, even though I still love the game."

"You're more than just the game," Olivia whispers.

And for the second time today, a woman strikes me right in the heart. Olivia sees me. The real me. Not the trophies or the bank account or the façade the fans see. I want to bury my head in her chest and let her hold me. Let her tell me all the ways I'm still a man even if my body fails me and hockey has to be put in my rearview mirror.

But that sounds a bit like stripping away everything and bearing my soul to someone.

So instead I slide my hand under the skirt of her dress and find out what underwear she's wearing. At least this is familiar territory. "You just earned yourself another hochimama."

Chapter Nineteen

Olivia

"Care to share with the class why you're thirty minutes late and looking like the cat that got the canary?" Evie whispers as she hooks her arm in mine.

Roman and I have just arrived at the rehearsal late, as Evie noted, but it seemed unimportant to be here on the dot since we're not actually part of the ceremony.

At least I hope not. *Oh, god.* With the way Taylor attached herself to me last night, it's a terrifying possibility.

Dan and Roman exchange fist bumps while I shrug off my concern and lean in to whisper back, "*Two* canaries, I'll have you know."

I can't help the guffaw that bursts forth at the look on her face.

"Did you just beat me at my own game?" my best friend asks, mouth agape.

"Seems I'm learning a lot of things on this vacation." I

wink, and her expression turns to a proud mama's on graduation day.

"Babe, let's get a round of drinks," Dan beckons his wife.

Evie lets me go to follow him but shoots a grin at Roman first. "Well done, Gretzky!"

"Do I want to know what that was about?" Roman lifts a brow at me, looking devastatingly handsome in a stylish white button-down he's left open at the collar. I could spend a week staring at that man's throat. Why have I never noticed how sexy Adam's apples are?

"Probably, but I'm choosing to leave your ego exactly where it is for now. If you pull a muscle at the buffet later, I might relent."

He chuckles and throws an arm around my shoulders.

We mill around chatting mostly with Holly and Dylan until Scott calls us all to attention. His outfit is direct from the Tommy Bahama "Midlife Crisis Collection," although I might be the only one who thinks so. It's impossible not to compare the casual ease with which Roman wears quality garments against the air of desperation Scott exudes.

Maybe I need wine. Where did Evie and Dan get off to?

"Thank you for coming, everyone," Scott addresses the gathering. "We've got a great evening planned, and some fabulous food and drinks to repay you for your continued patience with this overly packed week." A few people chuckle good-naturedly. "We truly appreciate each of you interrupting your lives to come celebrate with Taylor and me." He reaches for Taylor's hand with a warm smile and she takes it, snuggling into his side almost shyly.

I immediately feel like a bitch for my earlier thoughts.

"Now," Scott resumes with a squeeze of his gorgeous bride-to-be, "I've been told by my bride not to monopolize all the attention, so we'll go ahead and get started. We invite the bridal party to gather by the pergola; the rest of you are free to get drunk."

Taylor smacks Scott's arm and he laughs before dipping his chin to give her a peck.

The massive part of me that was dreading this week had feared moments like this—ones that would cause all the memories to rush to the surface and send me spiraling. Not that I have any doubt our divorce was the right move, but I was scared of the feelings Scott's wedding would dredge up in me.

Jealousy that he's found his perfect match? Resentment that he's still calling all the shots and the kids and I are forced to smile and go along? A stark reminder that with the kids gone and my body betraying me, my life is only downhill from here and there's nothing I can do about it?

But I'm not feeling *any* of that. I'm just feeling... relieved. Maybe even content.

Before I can examine it too much, Holly pipes up, "That's our signal, Dyl," and my kiddos head over to join the bridal party.

Roman laces his fingers in mine, bringing my attention back to him. "You doing all right?"

It takes no effort at all to give him a bright smile. "Better than."

By the time dinner winds down, Holly and Dylan have disappeared to rendezvous with Hannah and Chugger (whose real name I learned is Aloysius. No wonder he goes by a nickname). Melissa and Cassandra are both flirting with the bartender, and Evie and Dan are low-key making out at the end of the table.

As for Roman and me, I'm ready to head back to the bungalow and his expression tells me he is as well. Unfortunately, I'm beginning to fear he may have broken my vagina with all the action from our naked-vacation-fun plan. I'm in dire need of twelve hours of sleep and maybe an Advil.

Turns out sex *is* very much like riding a bike: when you haven't done it in a long time and you take a twenty-mile ride out of the gate, your nether regions are going to be sore as all hell.

Roman leans in to nuzzle my ear, and the full body shiver it elicits has me thinking of another fitting idiom: no pain, no gain. To hell with it. Life is short and mama's gettin' laid.

"Something tells me I won't be needing those blankets tonight," Roman murmurs. "But I think I'll go ask the front desk for another couple fans, yeah?" I feel his smile against my skin, and it makes me grin too.

"I'll go with you." I drop my hand to his thigh, and he stands from the table before we travel down Evie and Dan's path to PDA-ville.

"Olivia."

We both turn to see Scott standing a few feet away with a glass of Scotch in his hand and a relaxed smile on his lips.

"Hey, man," Roman greets him, but it's clear Scott wants a word, so Roman brushes a kiss on my temple before stepping away. "I'll meet you back at the room."

"Okay." I nod.

Scott watches Roman depart, but my eyes stay on my

ex, looking for any signs that I should be wary. I can't find any, so I step closer.

"He seems like a stand-up guy, sweetheart."

I want to bristle at his use of the old endearment, but I can't muster any scorn. When Scott's eyes finally come to mine, I know why.

He's happy.

For him. For me. For us.

"Yeah," is my only reply. I agree with him, of course, but I've also kind of pulled one over on Scott this week, and I don't want to imply more than the strict truth now. "I like Taylor," I confess.

"Don't take this the wrong way," Scott responds, but before I can get my back up, he continues, "but she's not you. I love her, and she's amazing, but there will only ever be one you."

My lips part, but I have no idea what to say to that.

"I fucked up." He shakes his head but keeps my eyes when he says, "I just figured it was about time to own up to it." Then he turns to face the path where Roman disappeared. "Taylor makes me happy, lord knows what I did to deserve it. And it's clear this Roman guy does the same for you." His eyes return to me–the same vivid hazel ones he gave both our kids. "I'm glad. You deserve someone who'll put you first in a way I never did."

His words are bittersweet, of course. His reflection on our marriage is monumental, and I take it in with all the gravity it deserves. He has no way of knowing Roman will be gone in a few days, though. Without thinking, I move closer and take Scott's free hand. "Hey." I give him a soft smile. "Did you see those two kids tonight?" His smile mirrors mine when he gets my meaning. "I'd say we didn't do half bad."

We're both silent then, and I let his hand drop before adding, "I had a hand in things too, Scott, so don't try to shoulder all the blame, okay?"

He doesn't respond to that, instead giving me a lift of his chin to acknowledge he heard me.

"I'm gonna head out," I tell him, and this time he nods.

But before I get more than a few yards, he calls out, "Turnabout's fair play, Olivia! When LaFontaine pops the question, let me know and I'll clear my calendar."

I chuckle and give him a wave over my shoulder. Then I take the path that leads to The Humpback and Roman.

What I don't do is allow myself to even think about going searching for unicorns.

Chapter Twenty

Roman

Despite getting less sleep than I normally would on vacation, thanks to a very relaxed-looking fashion designer last night with a mischievous twinkle in her eye that I couldn't dare disappoint, I feel like I could take on those twenty-year-olds looking to bodycheck the old man on the ice. I roll out from the mound of blankets on my side of the bed to stare down at Olivia all tangled up in a single sheet, her hair blowing in the wind. God, she's beautiful.

I didn't want to leave her alone with her ex last night, but she squeezed my hand like she had everything handled. When she caught up to me at the pier that leads to our bungalow, she was calm. No hint of tears or agitation from her encounter with Scott. I didn't ask her what was said, as it was none of my business, but she seemed far from the woman who showed up here earlier this week. No matter what happens between us when we go our separate ways,

I'll be grateful that I've been here for Olivia when she needed a confidence boost.

And now, she's going to be here for me. With an evil grin, I smack her on her butt. Olivia's reaction doesn't disappoint. She wakes up swinging, her fist connecting with just air thanks to my cat-quick reflexes. Her eyes hold murderous intentions, but she stills when she sees me.

"Really, LaFontaine?" Her voice is a sexy rasp so early in the morning.

"Time to work out, Ollie."

She flops back on the bed and tries to turn on her side. "You're the athlete. You do the workout. I'm going to sleep a little longer."

I go one by one and turn off all her fans. It sounds like a helicopter finally landing and shutting down its engine. Olivia sighs and comes up on her elbow to glare at me. "You don't play fair."

"Listen. I did some research last night during your thirty minutes of flip-flopping from one side to the other until you got comfortable enough to sleep." Olivia's gaze drops guiltily, and I have to bite back a laugh. "Regular exercise is supposed to be fantastic during perimenopause."

"Sounds like a lie a male doctor made up," Olivia grumbles.

I grab her hands and pull her up to standing, folding my arms around her. She's warm and oh so huggable right now in all her grumpiness. "It's true. Walking and yoga to relieve stress and achy joints. Weightlifting to keep on important muscle and prevent bone loss. You're coming with me from now on."

Olivia groans but doesn't fight me as I walk us toward the dresser that holds her clothes. "Fine. But no running. My boobs don't need that kind of bouncing and chafing."

I can't help it. The mental visual is too fantastic. I press my erection against her backside as I spin her around to get access to her drawers. Her head snaps up to look at me in the mirror. "Seriously? It's not even seven in the morning. How are you even awake enough for that?"

I waggle my eyebrows. "Can't help it. I want you all the time." I step back though and make my way to my suitcase to find a clean workout outfit. "If you're a good girl during our workout, I'll reward you handsomely when we get back."

It's not until I pull a T-shirt over my head that I feel Olivia's gaze on me. "What?"

She shakes her head, staring at me like I've grown a second head, which would be really unfortunate in my line of work. "I'm just trying to figure out what you've done to me. I'm waking up early to work out and actually want to jump your bones when just a week ago I thought that I might be a dried-up old woman who'd forever said goodbye to sex."

I grimace. "That would be a tragedy. Good thing you met me."

Olivia rolls her eyes and gets dressed. When she turns to me and spreads her arms wide, as if saying, "this is as good as it's going to get," I can't help but throw my head back and laugh. She's wearing a T-shirt with the words *I'm not arguing, I'm just explaining why I'm right*. Her hair is piled on top of her head in the messiest bun I've ever seen, and she's wearing no socks with her tennis shoes.

I open my mouth, but she beats me to it. "If you say one snarky thing about my outfit or my athletic abilities, I will march right back here and crawl into bed."

I make the motion of zipping my lips. "I would never."

And then we head outside to greet the sunrise with

some yoga, pushups, and walking lunges down the beach. When Olivia falls on a lounge chair left out by a nearby resort and declares her legs broken, I call an end to the workout. I'll get my run in tomorrow and let her sleep. I crouch next to her, insanely proud of her work ethic.

"Hop on, Ollie."

She lifts her arm and lets it flop down. "Can't. Everything. Broken."

I shrug. "Well, I guess I'll just have to tell Scott you couldn't come to his wedding this afternoon because you were too heartbroken about him moving on without you."

Olivia lunges forward. "You traitor!"

She wraps her arms around my neck and lets me pick her up, piggyback style. I pull her thighs around my waist and tell my overeager dick to wait his turn. We have to make it back to the bungalow before he can come out to play. In fact, he has a few hours to wait. I placed a couple calls last night while waiting for Olivia to talk to Scott.

I walk us back to the room while we chat about our plans once we're back home. I have games starting almost immediately and a few press events I've promised to attend. Olivia has a big software consultant coming to meet about expanding her custom scanning technology. Neither one of us talks about how all those plans require living multiple states away from each other. That this easy camaraderie we have will go away the second we go back to our real lives.

"What is this?" Olivia interrupts my thoughts.

I let her slide down my back and check out the massage table I had delivered to the room while we were working out. There's a stack of sheets and a bottle of the massage oil that Olivia loved so much from the spa our first day here.

"Your reward, my lady." I wave my hand to the table. "You shower and I'll get everything set up."

Olivia's head swivels. "The masseuse will come here to the room?"

I dip my head. "You can call me Sven."

"Wait, wait, wait. *You're* the masseuse?"

I approach Olivia slowly, watching the way her pupils dilate and her breathing picks up again the closer I get. Grabbing the hem of her T-shirt, I give it a little tug. "Shower, Ollie. Then I'll give you the best massage you've ever had. Believe me, I've had enough over the years to know exactly what you need."

She bites her lip, hesitating.

"Do you trust me?" If she says no, I swear I'll drop the massage idea and not even be hurt about it. At all. Totally. Not hurt at all.

"I do."

I swallow hard at those two little words. We'll be hearing them this afternoon at the wedding, but I try not to let them mean anything between us. "Then let me make you feel good. Let me worship this gorgeous body of yours. Let me get my hands on you the way I've been wanting to since the first day I saw you."

Olivia's cheeks have gone pink again. "You didn't like me that first day."

I shake my head. This woman doesn't get how beautiful she is. I dip my head so that I'm whispering in her ear. "Doesn't matter whether I liked you or not. I wanted my hands on your body. Now that I know you, I *ache* to get my hands on your body." I feel Olivia shiver at my words.

And thank the destination wedding gods, she moves away to take that shower. She comes out five minutes later with wet hair piled on top of her head and a white towel wrapped around her. I've got the sheet on the massage table and one for on top of her once she's laying down. I immediately tossed the blankets aside. Olivia would most definitely not want blankets.

She hesitates by the table for just a second. I lean in and kiss her cheek. "You just have to say stop and I'll stop. You hold all the cards here."

Olivia stares deep into my eyes like she's trying to solve a mystery. "That's far from the truth. But I do trust you. And I want your hands on me too." She lets the towel fall to the floor and climbs onto the table to lay down on her stomach.

My throat is instantly dry and my cock insists now is his time. Instead of listening to that joker, I drape the sheet over Olivia, leaving only her back exposed. The oil slides through my fingers, and I rub my hands down her spine. I lose myself in the sensation of touching every square inch of her. Her skin is like silk, every new bump and valley discovered makes me feel like I'm getting to know Olivia better than anyone on this planet. Her little shivers and moans are like catnip, making me crazy for this woman.

She turns over when I hold the sheet up and instruct her to do so. Her eyelids are heavy, and I pat myself on the back for making her so relaxed. But then my gaze drops and I see her fully naked and laid out for me. I hesitate, needing just one more second to gaze at her before I continue the massage.

"You're so fucking gorgeous, Olivia," I murmur, in awe of how lucky I am to have agreed to a fake date and wound up with someone like her. She's so much more than just a pretty woman. She's intelligent, successful, hilarious, and dedicated to her children. She's the type of woman you beg to marry, knowing you'll never be good enough for her. She'll always outshine whomever she's with because she's the complete package. She doesn't just slide a puck around the ice for a living, she makes a difference in people's lives.

"I'm starting to feel like I might be," she murmurs back, eyes closed. Her hands aren't trying to cover herself.

I drop my head to my chest and just breathe. That's the one thing that makes Olivia even hotter than she already is: confidence.

"You're killing me," I say on a tight chuckle, dropping the sheet over her and forcing myself to pump out more oil to finish this massage. I notice my hands are shaking, but I argue it's because I'm holding myself back from climbing up there and burying myself inside her tight heat.

Olivia smiles, her eyes fluttering open. Suddenly she whips the sheet off of her and I'm so very fucked. "Make sure you get that oil massaged into my breasts." Then she proceeds to cup them for me, like an offering I can't resist.

"Ollie . . ." I warn, standing stock still for fear I'll ruin this massage with what I really want.

"You said I get a reward for working out. I'd like my reward now." Olivia's eyes turn positively playful. "I need you naked though. Think this table will hold both of us?"

I kick my shorts off so fast I'm pretty sure they rip. My aching dick finally gets some attention when I use the oil on my hands to stroke it. Olivia watches, playing with her nipples. Goddammit. I put one knee on the edge of the table. "Only one way to find out."

Turns out the table lets out more groans than me, but it holds as I hitch Olivia's leg over my arm and slide home. It wasn't really built for this kind of activity, but I'm starting to believe that Olivia was built for me.

Olivia

"For someone who almost died this morning, I don't look half bad." I smile as I study my reflection, smoothing my hands over the robin's egg blue bias-cut dress that hugs my hips and breasts just right. Evie picked it out on our panic-induced pre-wedding shopping trip, and I kinda want to kiss her for it. I don't even care that the humidity will destroy my makeup before the I-dos or that my dress is two sizes bigger than those I wore when Scott and I were married.

"What's that?" Roman asks as he exits the bathroom.

"Nothing. I . . ." My words die on my tongue when I catch sight of him in the mirror. I turn to get a better look, and *wow*.

Roman stands by the bed in a wickedly fabulous navy linen suit, adjusting the cuffs on his crisp dove gray dress shirt that he's left open at the neck again. My tongue wants to trace the exposed hollow of his throat until he groans in my ear. His groans are as addictive as movie popcorn with Milk Duds mixed in.

It doesn't escape my notice that he's still not shaved since I told him how much I love his salt-and-pepper scruff. I have it on good authority that most hockey players grow beards as part of playoff superstition, yet Roman has kept his chin clean-shaven for the last few years. The fact that he feels comfortable enough with me to let it grow makes my chest warm and gets my mind moving in dangerous directions.

"You look *fantastic*," I tell him, not hiding my admiration one bit. Lord knows he hasn't been shy about his appreciation of me—stretch marks, tummy, and all—so there's no reason for me not to ogle him. "You should never cut your hair again," I tease because I love the way it brushes his collar and flips up at the ends in the back when it's damp like it is now.

He grins. "I'll take it under advisement." Then he steps closer, a very familiar look in his eyes. "Speaking of fantastic."

I throw my hand up between us. "Nope! It took the stylist an hour and a half to get me looking this good, and I'm not showing up at the wedding with sex hair."

"Then I need something else to keep my hands occupied." He grins.

"Here." I toss him my phone and he easily catches it before I turn back to the mirror so I can put on my earrings. "Text my mother to tell her I exercised today. She'll be thrilled."

"What's your password?"

"I was joking."

"You don't want me talking to your mother?" he teases back. "You're ashamed of me, aren't you? Am I nothing but your dirty little secret, Olivia?" His hand is over his heart now, making me laugh.

"I'm doing you a favor, believe me. My mother would love nothing more than to see me getting some for a change." I pause with an earring mid-air. "I take that back. She'd probably try to strongarm you into marrying me." I roll my eyes.

"It would save my mom the trouble." He shakes his head with a frown.

Not wanting to linger on this topic, even though I'm the one who brought it up, I quickly secure both earrings and turn to Roman again. "Ready?"

He crooks an arm for me to take, and even I can admit we make quite the dashing pair. "Let's tear it up, Ollie."

I manage not to cry—barely. And it's not because of Scott and Taylor, who both look radiant and happy, but because my kiddos appear so grown up. Dylan cuts a tall, handsome figure in his tux and neatly combed hair, and Holly is stunning in her sunset orange bridesmaid dress, her hair curled into an intricate updo to match the other bridesmaids.

As we sit in white wooden chairs watching the wedding party walk back up the aisle, I sigh and unconsciously rest my head on Roman's shoulder. It's so natural, I don't question it, and neither does he, apparently, because he gives my thigh a squeeze in return.

"Thank god. I'm starved," Hannah says from Roman's

other side. She's wearing a pink floral sundress that would look terrific with the latest Livvies sandals. I make a note to have Ashley get her started on the complicated custom-fit process so Hannah gets those shoes I promised.

The happy couple has put us at a table with Evie and Dan, as well as some of Taylor's family we haven't met yet—an older couple named Doug and Gloria and sister-and-brother cousins who all just flew in last night to catch the main event.

"I can't possibly eat another bite," Natalie, one of the cousins, groans as she leans back in her chair and pats her flat stomach over her silky dress. It's clear she and Taylor are related, as they share the same blond hair and similar bone structure.

"Airplane bloat," her brother, Trent, shares with the rest of us, causing his sister to straighten and smack him on the arm. "Happens every time."

"Shut it." Natalie frowns at him and then makes a move that has me struggling not to laugh out loud. Her half-lidded eyes slide to Roman before she pouts and says, "You'll make Roman think I'm a pig," causing Evie to lose the similar battle to mine she was waging.

Either Roman is oblivious, or he's on to Natalie and taking the path of least resistance as he responds. "Of course not."

Natalie laps it up, despite its lack of any substance, and I'm pretty sure the sound I hear is her purring.

Thank god the waiter comes to refill our wine at that very moment. It takes effort not to chug my sauvignon blanc while I watch Natalie eye-fucking my date.

All attention shifts to the small dance floor as the music gets louder and the newlyweds share their first dance. Scott smiles through the entire song, unable to take his eyes from Taylor. It's sweet.

Natalie is not the only one done eating, as most of the younger generation ditches their tables and gathers on the dance floor when the deejay switches to a Bebe Rexha song. My foot taps to the beat, and I know I'll be out there myself before long. I can never resist an opportunity to dance, but I'd like to hold off until a little later in the evening since I'm already warm and I know I'll get sweaty out there. That, and I'm guessing Roman's not a huge fan of the dance floor.

"Oh, I love this song," Natalie pipes up, throwing her napkin on the table and rising from her chair to join the small gathering on the floor.

My relief at her exit lasts only a few seconds, however, when she positions herself mere feet from our table and I realize this is all part of her seduction plan.

"Here we go," Trent mutters under his breath while Gloria diverts Roman's attention to ask him something about Tampa.

I, however, am unable to tear my gaze from Natalie as she somehow manages to pole dance without the aid of an actual pole—or the grace of an actual pole dancer.

Since Roman is otherwise occupied and Natalie is ruining this song for me, I decide to throw in the towel and get my groove on with Holly and Hannah on the other side of the dance floor.

Bebe switches to Calvin Harris and I'm lost in the music in an instant. I'm not the most graceful person on a normal day, but something about music makes my body and limbs work together in perfect harmony. Holly always teases me that dancing puts me into a trance, and I can't say she's wrong. It's the only form of exercise I can get behind because it's all fun and no work.

Hannah, Holly, and I move together through two more tracks before they beg off to get a drink and leave me by myself. I don't mind one bit until I notice a pair of hips beginning to gyrate a bit too close for comfort. When I look up, I see Trent dancing in my personal space, his eyes raking up and down my body as I move.

He's a good-looking guy, probably in his late thirties, with excellent cheekbones and a full head of sandy brown hair. In another life and another time, I might be flattered at his attention.

But that life and that time are not now.

As if I conjured him up from thin air, Roman appears at my side. He snatches my hand, turning me away from Trent and into him before he molds my body to his and begins moving with me in rhythm with the song.

"Every man in this place wants to fuck you on this dance floor," he growls in my ear.

Whatever reaction he's expecting is not the one he gets, which is me throwing my head back and laughing myself stupid.

His responding glare loses its bite instantly, however, when I wrap my arms around his neck and lean in to bite his earlobe and say, "I only have eyes for you, Ice Bath King."

Chapter Twenty-Two

Roman

The thud of Olivia's head hitting the sliding glass door has me coming to my senses. Barely. I wrench my mouth from hers to reach around and open the door before I give my date a concussion. Olivia's hands are squeezing my ass and we trip over our feet as we get into the bungalow. I'm not sure how we made it back here, but I'm glad we're finally somewhere private for the things I want to do to her. She drove me downright insane on that dance floor. We only made it through three songs dancing together before I literally dragged her out of there like a caveman to hoots and hollers from Dan and Evie.

Olivia's tongue is in my mouth and her hands are everywhere all at once. Usually I'm the one making all the moves to get in a woman's pants. I can't help but love the way it feels to be on the receiving end of someone being out of their mind to get a piece of me. Sadly, I have to stop her, or I'll have a mess in my pants like some kind of inexperienced teenager. I move quickly to snatch her wrists, pulling away from her momentarily.

"Turn around and put your hands on the dresser, honey."

Olivia swallows hard, little strands of golden hair pulled out of her perfect updo. I can see her beaded nipples through the thin material of her dress. Can practically smell the arousal emanating from her. I need to be inside of her. Now.

She turns, giving me her back and placing her hands on the edge of the wooden dresser just like I asked. My pants are officially painful. I kick off my shoes, tear off my socks, and let my pants sink to the floor with my boxers. My shirt is hanging half open from where Olivia started to unbutton it. I'm not sure where my suit jacket is and frankly, I don't give a damn.

With shaking hands, I unzip the back of Olivia's dress. When it doesn't fall off right away, I get frustrated. I yank on it and a loud rip echoes through the room. Olivia's head snaps up, but I'm too enthralled with the lack of a bra and the lacy underwear she has on to care about a dress.

"I'll buy you ten more, one in every color," I whisper in her ear.

My fingers trace down her skin, seeing the goosebumps follow. Her ass is right where I need it, thanks to the heels still on her feet. The satin ribbons that wrap her calves are the sexiest thing I've ever seen. My cock is running the show now and he's entirely too impatient for much more fore-play tonight. I consider the way she was moving her hips on the dance floor to have been the start of the foreplay anyway.

I squeeze my eyes shut and grab my dick roughly as I

put a condom on, hoping if I strangle it I can control myself a bit.

"What are you doing back there?" Olivia whispers over her shoulder

"I–" I drop my head to her shoulder to kiss her heated skin and restart my sentence, hoping I make sense when all the blood flow is elsewhere in my body. "I'm trying to slow down so I don't hurt you. I know you said things are more sensitive down there."

Olivia sighs like I've just whispered something sweet in her ear. Then she extends her arms and pushes her hips back. "Don't slow down, Roman."

I blink my eyes open and nearly swallow my tongue. She's got her legs spread and her ass in the air, inviting me to slide inside her body. And maybe I should check to make sure she's being honest, but I'm no longer thinking. I run my cock up and down her flesh, coating myself in her arousal and then plunge inside in one forceful stroke.

Olivia groans, long and loud. I still, wondering how something can feel so damn good you'd give up your whole life to get more of it. But then Olivia is mewling and shifting impatiently and I'm running on instinct. Her hips are in my hands and I'm pulling back out, feeling every inch of her and needing more. I slam back inside and Olivia begins chanting my name against her arm, where her face is currently buried. The dresser is hitting the wall and in the back of my mind, I know I'm being too rough. All I see is my cock disappearing inside of her and I can't stop the pistoning of my hips until I feel her tighten around me like a fist. Then she's whimpering and shaking, and I lose my goddamn mind. I should be more gentle, but I'm not. Another couple of thrusts and I'm spilling inside of her, holding on for dear life and draping my whole body over hers. I know I have legs but they currently aren't working and Olivia's grip on the dresser is the only thing holding us up.

Sounds and sensations come back to me after a few minutes of sucking oxygen into my lungs. I blink and realize I'm probably crushing her. I somehow let go of her and stretch to standing. Much more gently than I was going in, I pull out of her body slowly before scooping her up into my arms and carrying her to bed. She blinks up at me like I wasn't just an asshole, pounding into her like an animal.

"I'm sorry, Ollie," I whisper, settling into bed next to her.

She rolls her head and furrows her eyebrows. "Why?"

"I was...that was . . ."

Olivia smiles. "Amazing? The best kind of out-of-control sex ever?"

Relief rushes through me. "I didn't hurt you?"

She wraps my arms around her and snuggles deeper into my embrace. "Absolutely not. I might need a day to recover, but count me in for that any day."

I bury my nose in her hair and we fall asleep that way. No blankets, no fans, no hot flashes or insomnia. Just two exhausted happy people snuggling the night away. Thank god my teammates can't see me right now. I'd never live it down.

"Who cares if we're late? They kept us waiting for dinner the other night."

Olivia is rushing around the room, trying to slather sunblock on herself while also getting dressed and putting her hair in a ponytail. She's an adorable mess. "I know, but this is our one full day with them and I don't want to waste it."

I get it, but when she gets sunblock in her eye and starts running around the room in pain, I intervene. "Stand still, woman!"

Remarkably, she does, probably because she's in pain and can't see out of one eye. I finish rubbing in the sunblock all over her body, then help her step into shorts. She goes into the bathroom to wash her hands and I pull a pair of matching sandals out of her suitcase for her, along with a beach towel and the hat she wore on the snorkeling trip.

I don't tell her that I woke to find my suit jacket hanging on our bungalow door, along with a sticky note that simply had a badly drawn winking face emoji. It reminded me of being in college and hanging a sock on the doorknob to keep your roommate out when you brought a girl home. I'm pretty sure that delivery was the work of Evie, but so as not to embarrass my date, I didn't bring it up.

"Okay, I'm officially ready!" Olivia jams the hat on her head and spins in a circle to prove that she's finally ready for a day on a boat. "How did the kids find a boat? Hopefully it's big enough for all of us."

I put my hands on her hips and bring her in for a soft kiss. "I rented it and believe me, there's room."

Olivia eyes me suspiciously. "What did you do?"

I shrug and lead her out of the room, shouldering her

beach bag for her. "What's the point of having ungodly amounts of money if you can't enjoy it with others now and then?"

She scoffs and whacks me with the back of her hand. Then she spins on her heel and runs back inside to pee one last time. I swear she has the bladder size of a squirrel. We finally make it to the marina just south of the resorts without forgetting anything. Our boat is the biggest one out there, though calling it a boat is really understating it. It's a yacht. With five staff members to both drive this thing and serve food and drinks while we enjoy our day.

"Holy shit!" Dylan's voice comes from behind us, along with an excited squeal from Holly.

When we spin around, Hannah is smiling like she knows what I've done. I was the good-time dad her whole life, showing up with expensive gifts or taking her on exotic vacations. While I intend to be much more than that from now on, I can still be the good-time dad too. Right?

We set sail shortly after meeting the crew and the kids all claim loungers at the bow. Thankfully, they leave the two best chairs for Olivia and me. Smart kids.

"Did you put on sunblock?" Olivia asks all four kids.

Chugger proudly points to the stripe of white zinc on his nose while the other kids all groan. Olivia tosses them the bottle of sunblock she brought, always the mom. I didn't even think of sunblock. Then again, they're practically adults. They should know they need sun protection. Clearly my parenting style is more like my own mother's and less like Olivia's.

"Did you eat breakfast?" Olivia asks once they're all lubed up and relaxing back in the mid-morning sun.

"Yes, Mother." That was from Holly. Olivia frowns.

"I could use a second breakfast, not gonna lie," Dylan says, sitting up. Chugger fist bumps him in agreement.

"There's food inside. Help yourselves." Thankfully I know what being a growing man feels like and ordered catering accordingly.

Olivia hops up too, following the boys as they nearly run to the food. "I'm going to supervise. They could eat you out of house and home."

I watch her go, smiling at her concern. I've never met a woman like her. Most people start to annoy me after a while, but not so with Olivia. It's interesting. It's discombobulating.

"I've never seen my mom blush so often," Holly drawls, looking at me pointedly.

"And I've never seen my dad so obsessed with a woman," Hannah says, right on cue. As if this was a coordinated attack.

I hold up my hands. "Ladies. This is just an extended fake date. While I very much like your mom, Holly, this whole thing has an expiration date."

"It doesn't have to."

I sigh, knowing they're just echoing the same thoughts I've been having. "Well, her job is in North Carolina and mine is in Florida. Long distance relationships don't normally work out."

"But you said you're looking to retire soon. Right, Dad?" Hannah looks so hopeful it pains me to crush the ideas in her head about me and Olivia.

"Well, yeah, but I'm not sure exactly when that will be, and I can't ask her to wait. Especially not when we've only known each other a week. That's a big commitment. Nor do I even know if she wants a dumb jock like me. She's a successful, gorgeous woman who could have any man she wants. Preferably one who lives in her state."

"Have you asked her to wait? Because I bet she would." Holly and Hannah look at each other, nodding in agreement.

I open my mouth to argue, but Hannah beats me to it. "Daddy?"

My jaw snaps shut. Oh shit. She used the Daddy card. "Yeah, pumpkin?"

"I've never seen you this happy before. You're usually too busy getting back to hockey to even have a conversation. But you're different with Olivia. Please. Just talk to her. See if this can go anywhere before you write it off. Will you do that for me?" Hannah doesn't let up. "There's more to life than hockey, you know."

I gasp, infusing humor into a conversation that has me reeling. "How dare you!"

Hannah and Holly giggle like I knew they would.

"Promise me."

I hold out my pinkie finger and Hannah lifts hers from across the bow just like we did when we Facetimed each other when I was out on the road. "Promise."

Chapter Twenty-Three

Olivia

"I'm gonna move here," Dylan announces as he drops his head back on his lounger, looking like the classic tanned college spring breaker he is. Oh, the joys of youth.

"You'll have to learn Spanish or Kriol if you ever expect to get a date then," Holly reminds him from her own lounger.

He doesn't bother opening his eyes or turning to address his sister. "Nah, half the people here speak English, and from the hotties I've seen, half will do just fine."

"Said like a true American." Holly rolls her eyes and looks to me for backup.

I'm happily sipping some iced tea while we sunbathe at the bow of the ship, watching the water slide by and enjoying the gorgeous views. I know the doctor said caffeine only makes hot flashes worse, but what kind of monster expects a woman to survive without it? A glance to my right reveals Roman and Hannah talking to the captain in the enclosed bridge, the two of them listening with identical expressions. It's adorable. I know Roman said he and Hannah have struggled with their relationship, but from what I've seen this week, they certainly appear to be on the right path.

I look away to pin both of my kiddos with a mock glare. "No moving anywhere outside the southeast—preferably not out of North Carolina, but I'm open to negotiations if you have valid reasons."

"Then you're not going to like my plans to become a marine biologist and study tortoises in the Galapagos Islands." I know Holly is teasing, but the day will come when she well and truly flies the nest, and I'm not at all prepared.

"I consider all bets to be off," Dylan says, finally looking at us. "I've got a feeling a relocation might be in *your* future, Mom." At my confused expression, he clarifies. "I hear Tampa's not as bad as people say."

My mouth drops open, and I freeze with my bottle of iced tea halfway to my mouth.

Holly laughs. "Oh, come on. Don't look so scandalized. *Or* surprised that we can see right through you and Roman."

Dylan winces like he just tasted something foul. "I've become an expert at averting my eyes whenever you two are close. You're like Dad and Taylor, only worse."

"It's strange to feel like the prude in the room, isn't it, Dyl? Our parents are all grown up. Where did the time go?" She wipes a fake tear from her cheek. "Tear."

I grip my tea with both hands now and straighten in my chair as the breeze whips away at my hat. "I don't have the slightest idea what you're talking about. You're both well aware this was just a set-up for show. There's nothing real about it," I lie.

They look at each other for a few beats before throwing their heads back and laughing hysterically. I birthed a couple of prize smartasses.

I can only shake my head and wait for the hilarity to subside.

"Nice try, Mom." Dylan settles back into sun-worshiper pose with his eyes closed again—like he didn't just upend my day.

"You guys aren't fooling anyone; you're totally into each other," Holly gushes as she strikes a similar pose in her white bikini, her long lithe body perfectly relaxed.

"I . . ." I'm not sure what to say, so I don't say anything. If I admit to my feelings, the kids will only feel sorry for me when I get on that plane tomorrow. They're not supposed to be a shoulder for me to cry on—ever. That's *my* job.

"I think it's great," Holly doubles down at my speech-lessness.

"Ditto," Dylan seconds.

My eyes flash back to the bridge where Roman and Hannah remain—thank god. "I...I'm happy you approve, I guess? Roman is a very nice person, but don't read anything into this. The only time we plan to see one another in the future is maybe at Blue Ridge U's Parents' Weekends or possibly graduation."

"Are you serious?" Holly straightens in her lounger, propping her sunglasses on her head so she can spear me with a proper glare.

I meet her hazel eyes. "Perfectly."

"But... that's... crazy!" She throws her hands to the sides. "You guys are so great together! I've never seen you this happy."

My eyebrows spike because this is news to me. Did Scott and I really do such a horrible job at hiding our issues? I suppose I knew we did near the end, but before that? Ugh. Parent of the year award accepted.

"He's cool, and he's obviously a better fit for you than Dad. No offense," Dylan interjects.

"None taken," I mutter absently as this new information tries to sink in.

"You'd be crazy not to see where this could go, Mom. You're still young and hot—and you never date." This from Holly, of course.

"I mean, you're not *that* young." Dylan smirks. "But I hope I'm not hanging it up at forty-three. Just sayin'."

Holly snaps her gaze to him, settling her sunglasses back in place. "No, you'll be one of those disgusting ninety-year-old men who marry a twenty-year-old and have an end-of-life-crisis baby."

"You think? Thanks." Dylan visibly cheers at that, making Holly groan.

I shake my head at both of my kids. "Thanks for the compliments... I think. But you're forgetting Roman and I both have busy careers states apart. We have lives. We can't just ride off into the sunset and ignore all of that—even if we wanted to. Which we *don't*." I end on a firm tone.

It doesn't work.

"Why not?" Holly's eyes hold way too much determination for my comfort.

"Which part?"

"Why can't you ride off into the sunset?" She throws a hand up between us. "And before you even try to object, I'm ignoring the part about neither of you wanting to because that's a total lie."

I set my drink on the tiny table beside my chair and lean

in. "Because we're not teenagers, Holly. We're practical, level-headed adults. All the getting-to-know-you butterflies fade eventually, and then you're left with the everyday practical parts of life. Which means me in North Carolina, Roman in Tampa, and each of us moving on."

"So you won't even try?" Oh no. Are those tears welling behind her glasses??

My voice gentles. "It's not about that."

She proceeds to twist the knife. "You've always told us that failing is okay as long as we give it our best shot. But you're not willing to even give it a try?"

Well, shit. I knew my parenting lessons would someday bite me in the ass.

Dylan rejoins forces with his sister. "You should at least talk about the possibility with Roman, right? What do you have to lose? Like you said, you may not even see him again."

"I wouldn't bet on it," Holly murmurs. "Not if Hannah and I have anything to say about it."

Oh god.

"Holly, listen to me. I know you and Hannah have good intentions, but interfering in this will only make a mess. We're adults who need to make our own decisions."

She raises an index finger. "*Informed* decisions."

Again with my awesome parenting. Dammit!

"Meaning you have to promise to talk to Roman first." Her tears are gone, and it's all smiles now.

I sigh, knowing I've been beaten at my own game. "If I agree, can we move on to another topic? Like why Chugger has his face plastered to the bridge window?"

They both turn to follow my gaze and start laughing. Dylan picks up an empty soda can and hurls it at his friend, hitting him on the back of the head.

It seems I'm off the hook for now, but my belly is still flipping at the prospect of broaching any part of this with Roman. We agreed to vacation fun and no regrets.

So why does that sound like the biggest regret of my life?

By the time we get back to the bungalow, the sun is long gone and utter exhaustion has set in. The day was perfection, our two families melding with ease as we toured the waters surrounding the various keys and enjoyed decadent food and drinks throughout the day. Apart from the conversation with my kids, it was lazy, simple, and beautiful.

Roman was playful and affectionate all day, and I adored watching him interact with the kids, Hannah especially. He was entirely in his element, and I found it hard to stray from his side as I fed off his energy and basked in his attention. The day on the water was a perfect memory to take with me.

Neither one of us mentions this being our last night together, and I'm not ready to bring it up. My flight is at noon tomorrow since I need to get back to work, but the kids and Roman are staying an extra day to squeeze the last bits of fun out of spring break. I can't help but wonder if Roman will miss me. I hope he does. Which is both irrational and selfish, but there it is.

Because I know I'll miss him like crazy.

Wordlessly, I head to the bathroom to get ready for bed.

The dried saltwater has my skin feeling tight, and my hair is a rat's nest on top of my head, so I switch on the shower and give it time to warm up while I brush my teeth.

The bathroom door is closed, and that's intentional. I need a minute alone to gather my thoughts and make some decisions, and the fact that Roman doesn't stride in and finagle a joint shower tells me either he's passed out already or he needs a minute too.

The other benefit of showering alone is that I can shed some silent tears without having to explain myself. Like daughter, like mother.

When I exit the bathroom twenty minutes later, Roman is on the hammock outside. The instant he catches sight of me in his peripheral vision, his face turns soft and he slowly pulls himself up, eyes on me.

He's so handsome. And sweet. And fun. And sexy. And... *everything*.

I've never felt like I do when I'm with him. Could the kids possibly be on to something?

Roman shuts the door behind him and pauses when he reaches me. The backs of his fingers brush my jawline as he whispers, "I'll be out in a few."

To keep myself from going completely insane, I crawl onto the mattress with my phone and scroll through some emails. One from Ashley manages to distract me because it's filled with her usual overabundance of exclamation marks as she shares the name of our latest celebrity client. It doesn't feel too shabby at all to be in such high demand. Might be time to hire another designer.

Roman emerges in a cloud of steam like some hot superhero surfacing from a collapsed building turned to rubble.

"Um, c-can you switch on a fan?" I stutter.

He grins knowingly but does my bidding anyhow before approaching the bed in a towel, damp skin, and nothing else. I blindly grope for the bedside table to ditch my phone without spoiling my view of his body, but the device falls to the plexiglass floor with a thump and I could not care less.

Somewhere between his grin and his knee hitting the bed, he loses the towel. Then his body covers mine, only the thin material of my "Go Sportsball! Do the things and win the points!" T-shirt between us. The same one he hung his head in shame at just the other day.

How is it possible we've only known each other a few days? It's beginning to feel like we were meant to find each other, except that fate has an abysmal sense of timing.

Roman doesn't tease or cajole, and I don't attack him or even smile up at him. We're quiet and focused as our lips meet and our mouths melt together. The kisses are soft and unhurried, our hands lazily exploring one another's bodies until Roman slips my tee over my head. He worships my breasts with his tongue while I thread my fingers through his hair and savor every sensation like it's the last time I'll feel it. Because it is.

But I can't let myself think about that. Instead, I focus on the thrill of his teeth grazing my nipple and the pads of his fingers trailing down my thigh. My fingertips skim from his hair to the warm, firm skin of his shoulders, and I urge him back up to my mouth for more of his delicious kisses.

His fingers glide gently between my thighs to explore me with care until I'm wet with desire, and then he enters me so slowly it's pure torture. When I urge him with my hips, he only continues his leisurely pace until I understand what he's doing. Or at least I think I do.

He's making love to me. This isn't fucking or naked vacation fun; this is making love... and saying goodbye.

When I finally climax, I blame my tears on the physical reaction to Roman's expert ministrations. Even though I know I'm lying to both of us.

Chapter Twenty-Four

Roman

Yesterday was....well, it was amazing. And intense. I woke up this morning well before the sunrise, lying next to Olivia with my brain spinning. Yesterday felt like the exact life I would have chosen if hockey had never entered the equation. A beautiful, relaxing adventure with a stunning wife and a couple of kids. I never would have imagined that kind of life for myself, but the preview yesterday jostled something in my head. Now it's all I can think about.

Which is why I plan to talk to Olivia at the airport. Hannah is right. I need to put myself out there and see if there can be something more for us. There already is on my end of the fake relationship. I can only hope there's more on Olivia's end too.

"Ollie?" I call from the hammock. She's still not out and we have to leave in ten minutes if she wants to get to the airport on time.

I hear the bathroom door slam and take that as my cue

to help her with her luggage. She's not meeting my eye while she grabs her laptop bag, a neck pillow, a pair of sunglasses, and her phone. It's like I can see the shift in her from vacation mode to business mode.

"Got everything?" I ask, wheeling her bag to the sliding doors. This feels awful. Like skating out there on the ice knowing I'm hiding an injury and shit will absolutely hit the fan once the first guy bumps into me, but not being brave enough to turn around and stop this all from happening.

"Probably not," she snorts.

"I'll ship you whatever you leave behind," I assure her. Hell, if things go according to plan after my little speech I'll ship myself out to her.

We walk down the pier in silence, absorbing the early morning breeze and the birds chirping as they fly over the water looking for their breakfast. Olivia chuckles and I find her looking out at the water, a soft smile on her face.

"I feel like the day I arrived here was another lifetime ago," she says, seeing me give her a questioning look.

I grin, remembering meeting her. "You were a sweaty mess but still hot. I especially liked the see-through tank top thing you wore." I waggle my eyebrows and Olivia backhands my arm. "Man, you hated me back then."

Olivia slides her arm around my waist and puts her head on my shoulder. "I didn't hate you, I just couldn't stand how gorgeous and cool and collected you were when I was so frazzled."

I squeeze her tighter. "You think I'm gorgeous?"

She tilts her head up at me with a smile I tuck away in my memories. The sun is coming up behind her and bathing her in golden tones. "You know I do. Especially with that gray beard."

I kiss her, forgetting all about the suitcase I'm supposed to be pulling or the time ticking away before her flight. She melts in my arms, and I realize with sudden clarity that one last night together, one last kiss, absolutely none of that will ever be enough. I want all the nights. All the kisses. All the hot flashes.

I pull back just enough to look her in the eyes. "Olivia, I–"

"Oh look, the love birds are at it again!" Holly calls from behind Olivia.

Olivia spins in my arms, the spell broken. The kids are all there, still in pajamas, but awake early to hug their mother goodbye. Hannah comes to my side and I pull her close as Olivia says her goodbyes, promising to send care packages as soon as she can. Even Chugger gets in on the hugs and Olivia treats him just like one of her own kids.

"Tell her," Hannah whispers urgently.

"I was trying to," I whisper back. Raising my voice, I step away from Hannah. "Alright, kids. I gotta get your mom to the airport or they'll leave without her." Frankly, that sounds amazing, but I know Olivia has a ton of work to get back to.

They all wave and shout goodbyes as we walk to the front of the resort to catch the boat—and its chatty captain—to the mainland. I called ahead and had a rental car delivered to the dock for us. The valet stows her suitcase and I hold Olivia's door. She raises her eyebrows and I brace for teasing.

"A Bentley convertible? Really?"

I shrug and help her inside the luxury vehicle. "Again. What's the point of making all this money if I don't get to spend it?" I hurry around the hood and slide behind the wheel, making sure to tip the valet well.

"I don't know. Maybe give it to charity? Or to Hannah or her mom?"

I pull out of the parking lot and onto the street. "I do all of that, believe me. I make most of my money from brand endorsements and one hundred percent of that goes to charity. My hockey money is for me and my family." I give her a pointed look. "Which includes Hannah's mom. Even now that Hannah is an adult. I'm not an asshole celebrity athlete, I promise."

Olivia reaches over to squeeze my thigh. "I know. I guess the single mom in me gets her panties in a twist sometimes because not all baby daddies are like that."

It doesn't really feel like the right time to talk about a relationship, not when we are discussing exes and child support. Instead, we chat easily like we always do until we get to the airport. I park and get Olivia's suitcase out of the trunk. We walk hand in hand to the terminal and check her bag. My heart begins to race as we turn for the security checkpoint. It's now or never. Feels a bit like right before a game when adrenaline is high and there's a lot on the line. And thankfully, I was born for this moment.

"Olivia," I begin, tugging on her hand and turning her to face me.

"Oh, my god, is that you, Roman?" A feminine voice interrupts me yet again.

Olivia and I turn to see a well-dressed woman barreling down on us. Or me, specifically.

"Kaitlyn Phillips," I say with a genuine smile.

I'm not happy to be interrupted when I'm trying to pour my heart out to Olivia, but Kaitlyn is a sports agent who's damn good at her job. If I were just starting out in my hockey career, I'd choose her with utter confidence. She's beautiful, which turns quite a few of the young male athlete's heads, but her brain is sharp as any agent I've ever seen. In fact, I've referred several of the new guys on the team to her.

She lifts her arms and we hug, her chin coming up to my shoulders in the sky high heels she's known for wearing. Her suit is probably more expensive than the ones hanging in my closet at home. She pulls back but gives me a million-dollar smile.

"I was just going to call you. How crazy running into you here."

I turn to include Olivia. "This is Olivia." I pause, wondering what to call her, but then smoothly move on when nothing comes to mind that won't cause chaos. "Olivia, this is Kaitlyn Phillips, an agent for some of the guys on the team."

The two women shake hands, but I can't help but feel like Olivia's smile is fake. Kaitlyn turns back to me, talking a mile a minute as usual before I can excuse us and have my private talk with Olivia.

"I wanted to reach out, but this is even better. I have some gossip I think you'll want to hear." Kaitlyn's eyes are sparkling, like she's about to offer me something I can't refuse. Knowing her, she's probably right. "It hasn't been announced yet, but I have ears everywhere. Mid Florida University is starting an ice hockey program. D1. New rink and state-of-the-art facilities have just been approved. And they need a coach staff."

Fuck. That caught my attention alright. "I'm not a coach, Kaitlyn."

The sparkles intensify. "Nope. But everyone knows you're an ice hockey legend on the brink of retirement. What's a better way to go out on a high than to slide right into a high-level collegiate program? You'd be helping start the whole department. Leaving your mark in the hockey world for the next generation. It's damn near perfect, Roman."

Olivia shifts on her feet and I'm aware of her every move. A week ago I would have jumped at this chance. I'd be sitting down with Kaitlyn hammering out a plan and calling everyone I know in the hockey coaching arena to see if this could happen. But it's not a week ago. I've fallen in love with a woman who lives in North Carolina.

"I'll have to keep that in mind," I say diplomatically.

Kaitlyn snorts softly. "You better think quick. Positions like that go before they're ever made public. Have your agent call me. We can work together to get you the interview this week. I'm technically on vacation, but you know I work twenty-four-seven." Her sharky gaze softens. "You've sent a lot of players to me over the years, Roman. I want to return the favor."

I reach out and take Kaitlyn's hand. "I'll call you tomorrow."

Kaitlyn beams at me before turning to Olivia and dipping her head as a way to say goodbye. Olivia makes a noise I'm not sure anyone hears but me. When I glance at her, there's nothing but vacant aloofness in her eyes. She drops her gaze and speaks to the floor in a hurried mumble. "I've got to catch my flight." And then she spins on her heel and marches toward the security line, her passport in hand.

"Olivia! Wait!" I lift my hand, but Olivia has decided to take up running after all. She's now disappeared around the corner in the roped-off area of security. I can't go in there without a passport and ticket. I mean, I could, but I'd make a scene and my agent *hates* when I make public scenes. Kaitlyn would have him on the phone before I got the invasive pat down by an overzealous TSA agent.

My hand lowers back to my side slowly. Shit. I can't believe she just ran off like that. No goodbye? No hug or even a "fuck you later"? Nothing?

"Did I interrupt something?" Kaitlyn's frowning at me, probably because I keep cursing, as if it's a magical chant that will make Olivia reappear.

My brain is spinning yet again for a solution, but there's nothing that can be done. That didn't go well. At all. But maybe I can call Olivia once she lands and make things right. Then again, maybe they did end just right. Olivia didn't exactly seem heartbroken to part with me. In fact, I'm pretty sure she flat out hustled to get away from me. That isn't the goodbye of a woman who loves me.

"Roman?"

I turn to Kaitlyn and put my hand on her shoulder, digging deep for the patience I need to be professional. "You just watched me crash and burn."

It takes her a second, but then understanding dawns. Her hand comes up to cover mine with a friendly squeeze. "I understand all too well. Why do you think I'm taking an exotic vacation all by myself? Sometimes we all crash and burn."

We stand there companionably for a few minutes, quietly watching people walk by, eagerly on their way to vacation or going home with healthy tans and souvenirs. When I feel like I can speak, I turn to Kaitlyn again.

"I'm sorry. I hope your vacation gives you the peace you need. Mine just complicated things."

She smiles, but it's laced with a sadness I also feel. "If you love her, you should go after her. Do whatever it takes to put it all out there. All she can say is no. And quite frankly, no is better than wondering if you missed an opportunity. Speaking of missed opportunities, call me tomorrow so we can discuss that coaching position."

And with that, she's back to Kaitlyn the agent, fishing her ringing phone out of her pocket and moving off to baggage claim.

I stride quickly through the airport, angry, for sure, but also hurt. I really did believe Olivia would be open to my suggestion about dating long distance until I'm officially retired. I thought I had a decent shot. But then she walked away without a backward glance, like this whole week meant nothing to her. It says a lot that I'm more concerned over the missed conversation with Olivia than the chance to take a prestigious coaching job.

The drive back to the dock is dead silent. I don't enjoy the luxury vehicle. I don't like the wind in my hair. And I certainly don't take in the gorgeous coastline. All I think about is why, at the age of forty-one, have I finally fallen for the one woman who doesn't even care about me enough to say goodbye?

When I reach the resort I toss my head back and laugh. Because it's either that or cry. And Roman LaFontaine doesn't fucking cry. Especially over a woman.

Chapter Twenty-Five

Olivia

My childhood best friend, Tammy, and I used to spend sleepovers in her parents' basement watching reruns of *The Love Boat* and *Fantasy Island*. We both wanted to be Captain Stubing's daughter, Vicki, and live on a cruise ship or, at the very least, disembark from a private plane to be warmly greeted by a dashingly white-suited Ricardo Montalbán on a private island.

While we suspected neither was likely to happen to two middle-class girls from Greensboro, there was one thing we were certain was within our grasp. It was a rule of thumb, after all. People who go on fancy vacations *always* fall in love and live happily ever after.

As I stare out the airplane window into white nothingness, I can confirm part of that is true. To my horror, I I did fall in love with Roman. But the happily ever after? That's just for cheesy eighties TV shows and storybooks.

Because seeing Roman engaging with the glamorous

Kaitlyn brought everything into sharp relief once and for all. Our relationship is never going to be more than a holiday fling, no matter the tiny sparks of hope I'd been harboring.

"Would you like something to drink?" The flight attendant startles me from my stupor.

I shake my head. "Um, no. Thank you." Caffeine will only make me hot and keep me awake when the only thing I want right now is to sleep for a week. I dutifully dig my water bottle from my purse and take a few swallows.

Though I can't possibly be upset with Holly and Dylan for encouraging my hopes, I wish they hadn't let their own minds go there. It's normal to want both your parents settled and happy, but I'll just need to continue showing them there's nothing wrong with being on your own. I'll work, take up yoga, join a book club, and maybe even get a cat. And I'll watch "White Lotus" again to remind myself that my vacation could have ended a whole lot worse than getting my heart broken.

I close my eyes and lean my temple against the cool plastic of the window shade, an image of Roman and Kaitlyn projecting itself on the backs of my eyelids. It's not that I suspect an attraction there—although they did look like they belonged together on the society pages, so who knows? The entire encounter impressed upon me how far apart our worlds are.

I'm a wardrobe-challenged engineer/owner of a fashion brand whose favorite work days are spent sitting behind a laptop on my quiet back porch. The only lunges I've done in the last year—besides my Roman-instructed ones earlier this week—were toward an out-of-reach bag of tortilla chips in the pantry. My hockey knowledge could safely fit inside a Ziploc bag—the snack size! And the last time I was interviewed in person for a press piece, I asked the reporter to hold my purse because I had to pee so badly I thought I might have an accident.

Not to mention all my recent struggles with my body and hormones. I'll forever be grateful to Roman for making me feel sexy and desirable and not like a dried-out old hag. But we're not meant to end up as anything more than a memory to one another.

He's got a life in Florida—whether he retires and gets that coaching job or sticks it out a few more years. His life is filled with famous people, glamorous women, relentless press, a grueling schedule, and a daughter he's just vowed to give his focus. Not to mention, he could have any woman he wants with a simple crook of his long index finger.

Gah! I can't think about that finger and all the things it can do!

I straighten in my seat and take a few chugs of my water. Thankfully, the middle seat next to me is open, so I'm not disturbing anyone with my fretting. With the cap back on my bottle and a full breath in my lungs, I exhale and force myself to begin thinking about the next chapter.

But I can't help the tears in my eyes as I close the one on Roman and me.

"Call for you on line two," Ashley pokes her head into my office with her signature dazzling smile.

It's Saturday morning, so it's a ghost town in here, but I wanted to come check on some test models and production designs I'd had to abandon last week for the wedding. We've got a software consulting team coming in on Monday, and I need to be up to speed and ready to hit the ground running.

"I told you you didn't have to come in, Ash," I remind her. "Go enjoy your weekend."

"Are you kidding?" She shakes her short pink pixie cut at me. "Zander is all up in my business, and I need my peace to edit photos for my Gram."

I'm somewhat proud of myself for not immediately responding with an inquiry into her grandmother's health. Instead, I ask, "How many subscribers are you up to now?"

"Followers? Forty-nine thousand, thanks to my in with this amazing shoe mogul." She winks. "But I'm working on subscribers too–it's a whole thing. Not to mention TikTok, Snap, YouTube–you know the drill," she teases and I roll my eyes as she races away.

She should be a vice-president or creative director, but she insists that being my assistant frees her schedule up for her true passion, lifestyle blogging. The woman knows herself, even at twenty-four, so who am I to argue?

I snatch the receiver from its cradle on my desk and hold it to my ear before pushing the button for line two. "This is Olivia." When the caller doesn't respond immediately, a flush rushes up my neck at the irrational hope it's Roman calling. Maybe he misses me as much as I miss him. Despite my promise to move on, the only things I've managed to do since I got home late last night are scroll through cat adoption websites and spend every second thinking about him.

When I picked up a decaf—ugh—at a coffee shop on my way in earlier, my brain was so full of thoughts of the man that I gave the barista Roman's name instead of my own. I had to chug it and toss the cup before anyone saw it, I was so embarrassed.

"Ms. Wylder?" a decidedly non-Roman voice asks, and I slump back in my chair.

"Yes. How can I help you?"

"This is Peter Bancroft from StyleWire magazine." I shoot forward in my seat again, my eyes snapping wide. StyleWire is the country's elite mash-up publication. They cover everything from fashion to music, sports, and tech. They've got to be right up there with GQ in circulation numbers. "I'd intended to leave you a message, but your assistant told me I lucked out and caught you in the office," he continues.

I quickly don my executive hat and pray for cool. "It's a pleasure to hear from you, Mr. Bancroft."

"Peter, please."

I acquiesce. "Peter. It sounds like I'm not the only one who works Saturdays."

"The early bird and all that. Listen, I wanted to feel you out about a possible article we'd like to run on tech in fashion. Word on the street is you're the one to talk to."

Holy crap!

Don't downplay yourself, Olivia! You're a badass executive. What would Roman love to hear you say?

"Let's say you have my attention, Peter."

Here goes nothing.

Twenty minutes later, I'm hyperventilating in a stall in

the women's restroom with wet paper towels shoved under my armpits and my head between my knees.

I'm unsure how it happened, but I appear to have given Peter Bancroft the impression that not only am I a tech genius, but I'm a savvy fashion goddess as well–and am ecstatically anticipating both the in-depth feature and sprawling photo shoot he and his staff will be planning in the near future.

One minute, I was giving myself a Roman-style pep-talk and the next I was flying by the seat of my pants and talking a bigger talk than I've ever had the guts to before. The train ran off the tracks, and I was all aboard all the way.

Shit!

I try pulling in a full breath to stop the hyperventilating and manage to fill my lungs halfway. Another couple tries and I get closer to normal breathing and further from passing out on the bathroom tile. While I have faith in the building's cleaning crew, it's still a place where people pee, after all.

"You doing okay?" Ashley's feet appear under the stall door.

"Yup!" My response is strangled.

"Did something happen on your vacation, Olivia?"

Oh, god. She's sweet *and* perceptive.

"No. I'm fine. I promise. Just an upset stomach," I lie. "I'm going to head home." That part is the truth.

What I need right now is perspective and a cold drink—preferably sourced from the Napa Valley region of California—and a pillow to suffocate myself with. Either that or a kitten.

Welcome home, Olivia.

Chapter Twenty-Six

Roman

The bang on my door wakes me up. I sit up in bed to see Hannah waving through the gap in the curtains I didn't bother to close when I came back from my midnight insomnia run. Now I know how bad Olivia feels when she can't sleep.

"Get up, lazy head!" Hannah shouts through the glass. "You already missed breakfast."

Swiping a hand over my face, I go to crawl out of bed, only to realize I'm not wearing a stitch of clothing. "Go away so I can get dressed," I croak, surprised at my own voice. When did I turn into a senior citizen?

"Ew," Hannah deadpans. "I didn't need to know my father sleeps naked."

I roll my eyes and even that doesn't feel good. "Go away then!"

"Okay!" she shouts, giving me her back and leaning against the glass. Guess she isn't actually leaving.

I creep out of bed and pull on the first outfit I can find. I give the shirt a whiff and smell the whiskey I was drinking like water last night after I said goodnight to the kids. With a grimace, I toss it aside and pull on a different T-shirt. The only clean shorts I have left don't match, but I almost feel closer to Olivia by wearing an uncoordinated outfit.

I slide the door open and Hannah tumbles into my room. The room that no longer feels like a fun holiday without Olivia in it. The room that mocked me as I stared at the ceiling all night unable to get to sleep.

"Jeez. You look rough." Hannah wrinkles her nose. "Did you leave any whiskey on the island for the other tourists?"

I grunt, and she laughs so loud it hurts my head. "You're evil under that innocent face."

"Oh please. You have all these fans and PR people around you that baby you all the time. The great Roman LaFontaine can do no wrong." Hannah snorts, tugging on my arm and forcing me to step outside where the sun is too bright. "What you need is some tough love."

"What I *need* is to get back to hockey," I say automatically, the yearning to return to my sport so natural it's like breathing.

Hannah stops abruptly on the pier, pulling me to a stop next to her. "No. Absolutely not."

"What?" I squeeze my eyes shut and then look again. I could have sworn there was steam coming out my daughter's ears.

Her hands go to her hips, and I brace myself. "That's what you do, Dad. Things get even slightly uncomfortable and you just bury your head in the ice."

I lift a finger. "That actually would be quite painful."

"Shut up!"

I snap my jaw closed and stare at Hannah. I don't think I've ever heard her shout at me. Roll her eyes. Hang up on me. Walk out of the room. Sure. All of that, but never a raised voice.

"You know, I used to look up to you. I thought you were the strongest guy in the world smashing up against the boards and checking other players left and right. You're a hockey legend to everyone else, but you're my dad. My hero. I thought you could do no wrong, but this trip has shown me that you're just a guy. Like everyone else. Weak."

She shrugs her shoulders and I want to grab her and shake her. "Excuse me?"

"You heard me. The going gets a little bit tough and Roman just slinks away and drowns his sorrows in whiskey and hockey. That's pathetic, Dad. You need to grow a pair."

I nearly swallow my tongue, part of me wanting to ground her for speaking to me that way. The other part of me is assessing what she said and not finding much wrong with it. And that pisses me off too. I open my mouth and then close it again. She's standing there defiantly, daring me to prove her right.

"Go ahead. Walk away. I know you want to."

The image of Olivia walking away from me at the airport yesterday flashes across my brain and I can barely breathe. Is that how Hannah felt every time I'd walk away from her and return to hockey? That I was choosing a sport over my own daughter? That she meant nothing to me?

With a gasp of emotion I can barely contain, I pull her into me, wrapping my arms around her and holding on tight. "No, Hannah. I'm never walking away again." My voice breaks, which accurately describes the condition of my heart too.

Hannah's arms come around me and she holds me just

as tight. We stand there for long minutes, making up for lost hugs. "You're still my hero, you know," she whispers.

"You should find another one. This one is pretty shitty," I whisper back.

She giggles and pulls back, tears in her eyes that match mine. "No. That was just the tough love I warned you about."

Admiration swirls in my chest. "Have you ever thought about becoming a hockey coach? That speech was epic."

Hannah laughs and threads her arm through mine. We walk toward the beach area where I've reserved a cabana for all of us for the day. "I'm glad you're not walking away from me, Dad, but I think you also need to not walk away from Olivia."

Pain slices through me, along with a tiny thread of embarrassment. I've finally lost my heart to a woman and she doesn't even want it. "*She* walked away from *me*, pumpkin."

Hannah points to my lounge chair, Dylan, Chugger, and Holly sitting on theirs already like they've been waiting for me. "Have you talked to your mom today, guys?"

Holly and Dylan share a look, but it's Holly who spills the beans. "Just got off the phone with her actually. Did she sound weird to you, Dyl?"

Dylan shrugs. Chugger nods his head. "Dude. She was way weird. My mom does this thing when she cries. Her voice goes way high like she thinks we can't tell she's crying. Your mom's voice was really fucking high."

I flop onto my chair, equally horrified to hear Olivia's upset and irrationally hopeful that her emotions have to do with me. "Did she say why?"

Holly snorts. "No, of course not. Mom never shares that stuff. When she and Dad divorced she put on this elaborate happy face all the time. Super annoying and so obvious." Holly swings her legs over her chair and leans toward me. "Can you please call her? She really likes you."

"I don't know, guys. Maybe she was just emotional over returning to work."

Dylan cracks up. "Mom? Emotional over work? No, dude. She's emotional over you, so if you could please give her a call and make things right again, that'd be great. Happy mom, happy son."

"I think the phrase is happy wife, happy life," Hannah interjects.

Dylan throws an ice cube at her from his drink. "I know the phrase, okay? I was trying to make it apply to our situation. Mom was happy with Roman this week. She deserves to be happy forever."

All four heads turn in my direction, the unspoken question hanging there. I think about what Hannah said about running away. Maybe I do bury myself in hockey because it's easy. Maybe there's a whole life out there I haven't built because I've been so wrapped up in a sport that's about to spit me out due to my advanced age. Maybe my most meaningful work is yet to come. Maybe Hannah was right and I need to grow a pair (still can't believe my own daughter said that to my face).

I spread my hands wide. "I'd like to make her happy forever, if she'll let me. So help me come up with a plan."

Their victory shouts draw the attention of everyone on the beach, but I welcome it. For the first time since I drove Olivia to the airport, I'm happy. Hopeful. And more than any of that, I feel like I did when I picked up a hockey stick for the first time when I was six years old. I feel like I'm on the cusp of something great. Something life changing.

By the time we have to leave for the airport that

evening, we've formulated a loose plan that involves a phone call and begging. I have a whole speech written down that sounds like each of the kids and maybe a little like me. I have the largest bouquet of flowers ordered to be delivered to her house in the morning. And yet, something just isn't quite right. I hope a bit of a nap on the flight back to Florida will somehow gift me with the missing puzzle piece to this gesture. I want to put it all on the line so that even if Olivia says no, I'll know that I did everything I could. I can live with zero regrets.

I send Kaitlyn's multiple phone calls throughout the day to voicemail, figuring I need to solve one problem at a time. It's on the drive home from the airport in Tampa that another idea hits me. I pull out my phone and call my buddy, Damon Whitley. We grew up down the street from each other, and played on quite a few hockey teams together in school. We lost touch once I went pro and he stayed behind in North Carolina. Amazingly, he answers.

"Roman LaFontaine. I'll be damned. To what do I owe the pleasure of your call, man?"

"Damon." I grin as I watch the lights of Tampa flash by my window. I'm not going to bury my head in the ice, like Hannah accused me of. I'm going to shoot the most important shot of my life, and it's going to be epic. "You got a minute?"

Chapter Twenty-Seven

Olivia

"I knew it! Liar, liar, panties on fire!" At the loud and entirely uncharacteristic greeting from Ashley, I pull my phone from my ear and stare at it for a full five seconds. Then I realize what's happened and bring it flush with my ear again as I resume transferring my laundry from washer to dryer.

"Ashley, it's Olivia," I inform her. "You hit the wrong contact." Instead of apologizing or being embarrassed, though, she laughs. Loud. And long.

When she's expended herself, she bizarrely says, "It's all over social media. The PR people already called me to schedule a meeting. They wanted first thing in the morning, but I told them you were booked solid with the consulting team, so they're bringing lunch at one to discuss strategy."

I stand frozen, a pair of wet cotton underwear hanging limply from my hand. "What on earth are you talking about?"

"Like you don't know!" She tuts like she's scolding a child. "Sneaking away for a tryst in the tropics with *Roman LaFontaine*. Here I thought you were languishing miserably through Scott's wedding, and you were dirty dancing with a hot hockey player the whole time! I mean, he's too old for me, but I can still appreciate him, objectively speaking."

"Oh my god." I drop the underwear and brace against the washing machine. It's Sunday morning, and I've managed to put off my nervous breakdown over the Style-Wire interview to get in a walk, some decaf, and my piles of vacation laundry. But this news from Ashley threatens to obliterate any calm I've achieved.

"Oh my god is right," she chirps. "The PR team is salivating over this; everyone loves a celebrity romance. *Swoon!*"

"Ashley—" I begin, but she cuts me off, oblivious to my dismay as her excitement carries her away.

"I'm forwarding all the links to you since I know this stuff isn't your forte. But if you feel like scrolling on your own, search 'hashtag-LaLiv.' You guys have your own portmanteau! I so want to be you when I grow up, Olivia. Le sigh. Okay, gotta run; my phone is blowing up." She hangs up without another word.

I blink a few times, attempting to absorb everything my assistant just threw at me. Roman and I have a *hashtag*? What the hell is going on?

Ditching the laundry, I stagger to my bedroom and flop onto the bed, thumbs to my phone as I prop myself on my elbows and open my email. Sure enough, there's a message from Ashley filled with half a dozen links.

I click the first one and gasp.

The photo is clearly from the wedding reception and shows Roman and me on the dance floor, his hips grinding into my pelvis as my arms circle his neck, my smile wide and open and directed right at him. His expression broadcasts to anyone within a five-mile radius that he's thinking about fucking me and might consider doing it right on the crowded dance floor.

If I weren't so freaked out, I might stop to consider we look hot together. But I'm too busy having a mini heart attack and sweating through my shirt in panic.

My eyes flash to the post wording to see a celebrity rag has shared an original post from a user named @ccmarkham88 and tagged Roman as well as my professional Livvies account—the one that Ashley mans. The text reads, "Is star Storm Chasers' forward officially off the market? Roman LaFontaine pictured here getting down on the dancefloor with Olivia Wylder. You may not know her face, but unless you've been living under a rock these last two years, you undoubtedly know her shoes. The creator of the much-coveted Livvies has clearly caught the handsome hockey star's eye."

"Shit."

I quickly scan the original post. "Had a blast at my little sis's wedding and even got to party with celebrities! These two make another perfect couple." When I look closer at the poster's avatar or whatever it's called, I recognize Cassandra, Taylor's sister. Her post tagged Roman but not me.

I click to investigate further, though, and see Holly has commented, "My mom sure can cut a rug! Go, Mom!" and tagged me. My groan gets caught in my throat when I see the post has been shared fifty times and viewed by over ten thousand people.

How could this happen? And, more to the point, why do people care?

Roman is even more famous than I realized, that's

obvious as I continue clicking on the links Ashley sent in her original email and the three others following it. People are going crazy, reposting and sharing this supposedly earth-shattering news about Roman's love life.

I've worked myself into a damn good fluster by the time I toss the phone down and drag my ass to the kitchen for a cold drink. My PR team thinks I've bagged a hotshot. This is so humiliating. What in the world am I going to tell them tomorrow? That this is all just a big misunderstanding? That I was only getting my rocks off on vacation while fake-dating my daughter's friend's dad to make it through my ex's wedding? I'll look like a complete and utter fool.

The truth can absolutely *not* come out; this is the kind of thing that can destroy a niche business like mine. I chug a glass of ice water, my heart thumping so loud in my chest I feel like I can hear it.

Think, Olivia! Think!

The entire thing was supposed to be simple. Save face in front of Scott and hang out with my kids. How in the world did that turn into such a gargantuan mess?

And what must Roman be thinking?! Oh god. Would he think I orchestrated this for publicity for my company?

No, he wouldn't think that. Would he?

Crap crap crap!

The ringing of my doorbell has me jumping out of my skin. Have the infamous paparazzi found me to quiz me about my affair with Roman? Do they know the truth already?

How does Roman live like this?

I tiptoe to the dining room and pull back the curtain an inch to get a clear view of the driveway. A flower delivery van sits parked in the drive but that's it. Hmm. Perhaps my imagination got away from me a tad.

I decide it's safe to open the door. "Delivery for Olivia Wylder?" The man reads from the card in his hand as he extends a huge bouquet toward me. It's bursting with coral roses, delicate pink plumerias, and the most perfect coral charm peonies all tied in a wide pale pink velvet ribbon. It's utterly fabulous.

I stutter a few words and accept the enormous bouquet before shutting the door and racing to the kitchen to read the card. It's idiotic to get my hopes up; it's probably from Peter Bancroft, a thank you gesture for granting the interview that I can't think about right now or my head really will explode all over my granite countertops.

My hands are shaking as I pull the card from the envelope.

We need to talk.

XX,

R

What the hell does that mean?!

"Didn't we just do this a month ago?" Evie asks from her usual chair opposite mine at my kitchen table. Roman's bouquet and card, with its cryptic message, lie on the table between us.

"Maybe I should move. At least that would mean no more mind-fucks appearing at my door."

"I'm certain this isn't meant to mess with your head. He obviously wants to pursue this thing with you, not get together to go over your expense report."

"I've changed my mind." I sweep my hands out, almost knocking over my water. "Let's talk about you instead. Have you signed that client yet? The one who refers to his Dobermans as his 'beloveds'?"

My stall tactic doesn't work; I know this when Evie gives me her version of resting bitch face, which is so far from actual bitch it's funny. But at least she tries.

I give in. "He's upset about all the posts." Of course, I shared the posts with Evie immediately. Instead of finding them alarming and a bit terrifying, she thought the whole thing was *cute*. She also thinks my concern over my company is nuts.

Cocking her head, she expertly switches to her 'are you high?' look. "What about these expensive-ass, romantic flowers says anger to you? Wake up, woman. You're hot, he's hot, you're both hot for each other. End of story."

I fiddle with my water glass and bite my lip as I consider this. Our time in Belize could certainly be characterized that way, given all the evidence at the time. But it's over, isn't it? Practicality and all that?

Evie gestures to the flowers and continues, "This clearly isn't about social media posts or being upset. Angry people send emails littered with manic typos. Either that or they leave nasty voicemails. Or bags of flaming dog poo on your front porch. Or they hide behind their keyboards trashing you online and tagging your boss because people are petty AF. Or sometimes—"

"I get the picture," I cut her off. She smiles and causally sips her coffee.

"I can only pray Roman doesn't spill the truth about posing as my boyfriend. I've already texted the kids begging them to keep it zipped. Although, from the photos and posts Holly has made, she's clearly still holding out hope for hashtag-LaLiv." My forehead hits the table on a groan.

Evie reaches over and pries my face from the table. "She's not the only one."

"Evie, the scene at the airport was not pretty. I can't believe I was even considering asking if he wanted to pursue something more. For one, he's either retiring and taking a hot-shot coaching job or playing a few more years—either way, he's in Florida and his schedule is packed. And two, he probably has a girl in every port, so to speak. The notion of letting things ride and seeing what happens was never even on the table."

She only shrugs and flips her dark hair over her shoulder. "I say you hear the guy out. What harm can it do?"

My heart is already broken, but hearing his voice again could shatter it into even finer pieces—shards that will cut like glass. Of course, I can't tell her that. Who falls in love over a fake date and a few nights?

"You know, this isn't exactly the Oregon Trail."

My brow knits. "I know my focus hasn't been stellar lately, but did we just switch topics entirely?"

Thankfully, she explains, "You don't have to travel by wagon train to see one another—it's not even a two-hour flight to Tampa. And you can take your time to see if it works out. The fate of the world doesn't hang on you two riding off into the sunset tomorrow or repopulating the earth with his super-sperm." She does the impossible and makes me grin.

"His super sperm?"

Her coffee mug clunks to the table. "Have you seen him play hockey?"

"No." Something delicious curls in my belly at the

thought. I'm so easy. The man can drive me to distraction even when he's a couple states away.

"Then you are in for a treat, my friend."

"Is he really that good?" I go for casual and fail if Evie's expression is any indication.

Her chin dips and she eyes me. "Is Yume the best ramen place in Charlotte?"

My eyes widen. Yume's ramen is sacred to Evie and me. We go there at least twice a month.

Evie snatches my phone from its spot by the note and holds it out to me. "At least text him and thank him for the flowers. We both know it's physically impossible for you not to exercise the most basic of manners, at the very least."

I sigh and take the phone from her, knowing she's right and mentally tugging up my middle-aged girl panties.

Welp, here goes nothing.

Chapter Twenty-Eight

Roman

My fucking back feels like I got punched in the kidneys, my knee is screaming again because I didn't work out nearly as much as I should have in Belize (unless you count orgasms as workouts, in which case I won a goddamn gold medal), and my entire focus is on getting to my phone after practice to see if Olivia texted or called. The flowers should have been delivered by now and I'm hoping for some contact. Some tiny sliver of hope that everything I'm about to do is not for nothing.

"Hellooo?" Banks waves a hand in front of my face, his voice higher than Mrs. Doubtfire.

I blink and shoot him an eat-shit-and-die look. He knows I love him. And that he irritates me equally as much. "What? I tuned out about the time you started talking about the redhead's dress."

Banks shoves my shoulder and flops down on the

bench, leaning on the front of my locker. There go my plans for grabbing my phone first thing. "I'm sorry. Am I making you jealous with all my recent conquests while you were hanging with Hannah on some remote beach?"

"Yeah, that's it," I say dryly.

"You should not speak of women this way, Banks." Niko Drugov, the Storm Chaser's best goalie, comes to my rescue, frowning at Banks in that way of his that leaves even the biggest guy with a shiver of fear up his spine.

Banks tosses him an easy smile that works on everyone, no matter their gender or inclination towards grumpiness. "Ah come on, Druggy. I was just playing around. You know I'm all about consent."

Niko throws his pads in his locker, briefly touching the photo of his daughter he's had taped there since she was born six years ago. "You must stop with that nickname."

Bobby Rhodes, a new player with a ton of potential and not one lick of social etiquette sense in his young brain, pushes himself into our tight circle. "Hey old men crew, what's hanging? Besides your balls." He tosses his head back and laughs his ass off. Fucker. I'll have to check him next practice to remind him I may be aging, but I've got two decades of evading the notice of the referees.

"Why you be staring at our balls like that, weirdo." Banks gets up to bump chests with Bobby, leaving my locker free finally.

I lunge for it, not giving a shit about the same old hazing we give each other every single day. I grab my bag and slide out my phone. Instead of a text from Olivia, there's a thousand notifications on my screen. I scroll through, not understanding what's happening, but zeroing in on the ones from my mother. For a split second I wonder if my secret got out before I'm ready to announce it. Then the first link Mom sent loads and I see a picture of my hot fake girlfriend, her hands suspiciously low on my back. I know that exact moment. We were dancing at the reception and Olivia grabbed my ass. Two seconds after that, I dragged her off the dance floor and took her back to our room where she grabbed it some more.

> Mom: FAMILY DINNER AT MY PLACE. BRING YOUR GIRLFRIEND.

> Me: Whoa. Slow your roll, and for God's sake, take off the caps lock. Very hard on my aging eyes.

> Mom: I wouldn't have to text-shout if my own son kept me up to date on his life.

"Holy shit!" Banks's loud voice interrupts my responding text. His head lifts from his own phone just a few lockers down from me. He looks right at me, eyes dancing with humor. "Looks like you still got it, old man!"

Then the locker room erupts, every player who has my back on the ice giving me shit for going viral on social media with a relatively unknown woman from North Carolina. Pictures of our vacation together are passed around and I'm having to hold myself back from punching each guy who talks about Olivia's luscious body. By the time Dave Wainwright, our team's assistant coach bangs his hand on the side of the lockers to get our attention, I've taken five orders for custom Livvies for girlfriends and wives. The fact that I can't promise them anything until I talk to Olivia doesn't seem to faze them.

"LaFontaine. My office." Dave spins right around and leaves the locker room to the hoots and hisses from my teammates.

"Oh shitttt. Roman's in twouble," Bobby whispers loudly enough everyone can hear.

I roll my eyes, make sure my phone is in my hand, and walk out to find Dave. He's already in his little office, pointing at the single chair opposite his. I sit and try not to feel like I'm in the principal's office. I did nothing wrong, but this isn't how I wanted management to find out about my plans.

Dave holds up his hands before I can speak. "I'm not upset. Nothing wrong with the photos that were leaked. But Olivia Wylder is not some puck bunny."

"Damn right she isn't." I don't even want her name in the same sentence.

Dave gives me a look that says to settle down. "Whatever this is, a relationship or a fling, will this affect your play?"

I shake my head. "Hell no."

I force my mouth to close before I spill how I really feel. If this thing with Olivia is reciprocated, it'll not only affect my play, it'll trigger some big changes. But that's a conversation I need to have with management all together. I decided the last few days that no matter what happens with Olivia, I have some big changes in front of me. Feeling like every joint was on fire during practice today confirmed it.

Dave dips his head and I'm free to go. He trusts me to do the best thing for the team and I respect that. I don't even make it back to the locker room to shower and slide into my ice bath before my agent, Jim Slovak, whacks me on the back and pulls me aside.

"What the hell are you doing here, Jimmy?"

He's dressed impeccably, like always, a neat little pocket square matching his socks. The man must sleep in a fucking suit. "My best athlete is in the news. Where do you think I'd be?"

I frown. "Is it really that big of a deal?" I've been photographed with women before. I don't see why everyone is getting excited over this.

Jim shakes his head, smiling like I'm a naive little kid. "It's Olivia Wylder. The relatively unknown face behind a super trendy brand. And she's your age."

I roll my eyes and run a hand through my sweat damp hair. "I date women my age all the time."

Jim lifts an eyebrow, but lets that comment go, dipping his voice like he's handing off state secrets. "Fans are eating this up, Roman. You need to renegotiate your contract after this season. As the oldest guy in the league. What's more youthful than falling in love?"

I don't bother to whisper my reply. "I won't use Olivia."

Jim steps back. "Who said anything about using? You at least like the woman, I assume?"

I nod.

"Then let's get more pics with her. Drip them out, keep the fans raving. Sit down at the negotiating table with momentum behind you. You need to seem younger than you are, Roman. In fact, you need to be showing up even earlier for extra skate time. Longer workouts. If you want another year or two you need to be all in on every front. Management needs to know you can handle another season."

I'm exhausted just listening to him. My phone vibrates in my hand and I look down to see a text from Olivia. My heart takes off as if I'm in the middle of that extra skate time. "Gotta go, Jim, but I'll keep all that in mind."

I head back to the quieter side of the locker room, slipping into the ice bath while all those young fuckers don't bother with recovery modalities. I have to grit my teeth against the white-hot pain before I allow myself to read the text without distraction.

> Olivia: Thank you for the flowers. They make me smile. I agree that we need to talk. My PR team is freaking out.

I drop my head and then whip it back when my nose dips into the icy water. Shit. I didn't even think about how her own PR team would feel about the leaked pictures. Maybe they're more conservative than hockey, frowning upon these kinds of things. It's not the reason I want her to talk to me, but I'll take what I can get.

> Me: You have the world's best smile. I hope the pictures don't cause trouble for you. Tell you what…I have a game in South Carolina tomorrow night and then we'll be up in North Carolina two nights after. How about we talk in person?

> Olivia: I'd like that.

I shove my fist in the air and let out a shout.

Fuck yeah. I'll be seeing Olivia in just a few short days. Stepping out of the ice bath, I wrap a towel around my waist and prepare to bring in the big guns to execute my plan. But first I need to get dressed and have a tough talk with management.

Hockey's been good to me, but it's time I'm good to

myself. I simply want more. After intense discussions with Damon, head athletic director at Blue Ridge University, this week, I can confidently say that North Carolina is where all my "more" is.

Chapter Twenty-Nine

Olivia

My envisioned coffee date with Roman to assess his state of mind over the whole social media blow-up (and possibly engage in some flirting and who knows what else) is quickly commandeered by Holly and Hannah—purportedly, with Roman's blessing. He wants face time with Hannah while he's in town, so any illusions I might have had about an intimate get-together are quickly squashed. His text about my smile had me hoping, but a crowded hockey arena is not the setting anyone would pick for some alone time.

This means the kids are coming to Charlotte for Roman's game, and we're all to be treated to gratis tickets to the Storm Chasers v. Silverkings matchup, after which I assume I'll get a few minutes with Roman. It's not much, but I'll take it.

Any way it goes down, it obviously requires a shopping trip with Evie to outfit myself appropriately. And since I've never been to a hockey game in my life, I need all the help I can get. I'm informed by my best friend that jeans are the only way to go, which presents a problem since no woman on earth enjoys the nightmare that is jeans shopping.

On approximately the forty-ninth pair, we hit a winner, a pair of slim-fit dark wash Stella McCartneys that cost half my paycheck but hug my hips and lift my ass in a way that makes them worth every cent. We pair this with a fitted cashmere sweater in Storm-Chasers gold that dips low in a vee that's just this side of decent. I have no idea how Evie talks me into it, but at least I have the option of a scarf for modesty, assuming the arena is cold. But what do I know?

Hannah and Holly show up at the house early with Dylan in tow, Dylan in a big gold hoodie and the girls wearing oversized Storm Chasers jerseys with "LaFontaine" and the number thirty-seven on the back. The girls take more than a passing interest in helping me get ready for the game. And It doesn't occur to me to suspect anything might be up because my nerves are already jangled at the prospect of seeing Roman for the first time in almost a week.

I miss him. I miss his scent and his smile and the deep timbre of his voice. I even miss him teasing me and calling me Ollie. And I miss his arms, his kisses, his cock, his groans, all of it.

Maybe this is a mistake. The way to get over a guy is not by getting dolled up and going to watch him skate around getting sweaty and flexing his muscles!

By the time we get to the arena, my stomach is sprouting a butterfly colony and I'm hot as hell due to the warm clothes on a sunny North Carolina spring day. But at least I look good. The girls did a bang-up job on my hair, taming it into soft curls that brush my collarbone, and they stuck mostly to my edict on natural make-up, although even I have to admit the red lip is killer–and immune to perspiration.

"Are we early?" I ask, glancing around and noticing for the first time that the crowd is sparse at best.

"Tickets for LaFontaine," Hannah announces to the teller at the will-call window instead of answering me. She slides her ID across the counter with a smile and a flip of her blond hair, and I decide to just wait it out.

The teller quickly passes an envelope to Hannah, instructing us where to go. When I drape my scarf around my neck, Holly swipes it from me in one stealthy motion and shoves it at Dylan who stuffs it in his sweatshirt pocket.

"That's my scarf!"

"You look better without it, trust us," Hannah answers for my daughter as I narrow my eyes at both of them.

I have no choice but to follow the kids to what I assume are our seats. It's not exactly freezing in here, I suppose. In fact, now that we're farther inside the building, the cooler air feels fabulous against my exposed skin.

A stern-looking usher holds a hand up to stop our troop, and Hannah passes out lanyards holding big plastic cards with official lettering declaring us VIPs. Good lord.

"Here. Put these on."

"Excellent." Dylan tosses his over his head and saunters right up to the usher. We all follow suit, Holly only pausing to roll her eyes at her brother and Hannah to show our tickets to the usher.

My heartbeat thrums in my ears as we pass through another set of ushers and are led right down to the rink and into a row of seats behind what I'm assuming is Roman's team bench.

"Holy shit. These seats are tight," Dylan exclaims,

shifting down the row to grab his seat in the middle. Fans are trickling in, but the arena is only a third full.

I take my seat next to Holly and lean over her to ask Hannah. "Why are we here so early?"

Her grin is a little more evil than I'd like when she points to the ice and says, "That's why."

When I follow the direction of her finger, my breathing stops for several seconds as a crowd of Storm Chasers and Silverkings decked out in full uniform, sticks in hand, take the ice. And by take the ice, I mean TAKE IT. They're not only fast and agile, passing pucks around with ease, but they're graceful. These big guys defy physics. It's almost like dancing the way they glide and pivot, working their sticks like they're an extension of their bodies and leading the pucks as if invisible strings tether them to their sticks.

It's incredibly masculine, but also beautiful. That is, until they all start slapping the pucks and pummeling the poor goalie. Pucks are flying everywhere, and snow showers of ice spray left and right. My heart rate continues to climb.

"There he is!" Holly shouts, bouncing in her seat. "Go, Roman!" she shouts just as Hannah cries, "Go, Dad!"

I can't tear my eyes away as Roman's neck twists our way, and then I'm pretty sure I have a small orgasm when his eyes find us, that sexy mouth widens into a full-blown smile, and he throws us an unbelievably cool chin lift. I notice immediately that he's kept the beard.

Oh. My. Ovaries.

Both girls are shouting as Dylan snaps pictures with his phone and the team warms up. But it's over almost before it begins, and both teams skate off the ice and disappear through the same tunnel from which they emerged only minutes before.

"This is so exciting!" Holly grips my arm and shakes it. "Aren't you excited?"

"Absolutely." She doesn't need to know the direction of my particular excitement, however.

I can't believe it took me forty-three years to realize that professional sports can be such a freaking turn-on!

By the time the arena fills and both teams are back on the ice, I'm riveted. When Roman doesn't single us out again, Hannah leans over Holly for some reason to say, "He's in the zone now. He needs to focus on the game. We'll get to talk to him after."

All I can do is nod. Why she thinks I need reassuring is beyond me, but I won't lie; it feels good to know.

We spend most of the first period on our feet cheering the Storm Chasers on. Our goalie, Niko Drugov—and I say "our" because I decided to become a lifelong fan of the Florida Storm Chasers the minute Roman's eyes caught us behind his team's bench—is pretty much a magician, twisting this way and that, throwing himself on the ice, and intercepting pucks flying at lightning speed.

But, of course, nobody catches my eye like number thirty-seven. Roman skates like the devil is chasing him, and his stick handling is so dizzying I have trouble following the puck half the time. Despite his obvious talent, as well as that of all the other players, the game is scoreless going into the third period.

Dylan and the girls have made two concession trips so far, but my eyes haven't left the game once. Every time Roman gets on the ice, shivers of desire thrill down my spine and my breath catches. I even caught myself panting during a particularly tense moment where he dueled for the puck and came out the winner, deftly outmaneuvering his opponent and racing down the ice toward the goal.

And it's not much better when he's on the bench directly in front of us. His attention remains on the ice at all times, but the frisson of awareness on my end is like a giant zap of lightning whenever my eyes catch on the revealed skin of his neck or the way his hair curls at the ends with sweat. I'm pretty much the definition of a hot mess.

I also really need to pee and have had to do so since the middle of the second period. And because this is the last break, I have to make a run for it and just hope I don't miss a second of play. However, I'm not the only one with that idea because the line at the ladies' room is never-ending.

After ten minutes, I reach a point of desperation and decide the hell with it. I march my butt into the mostly empty men's room, eyes cast down until I'm safe in a stall. Business done, I race back to our section, but as I'm shuffling down the stairs to our row, I see the game is already in progress and Roman is racing down the ice toward the other team's goal. He passes it to a player named Banks on the opposite side of the ice and skates around a defender just as Banks sends it back.

Roman wastes no time, drawing back his stick and slicing the puck directly through the miniscule space between the goalie's knees. The arena erupts with groans and cheers alike just as I reach our row. The girls are jumping up and down, screaming their heads off. Dylan is hooting through cupped hands, and all our eyes go straight to Roman as he glides back toward center ice, hands raised in victory and his teammates attacking him from all sides.

I feel like my smile might break my face as I throw an arm around Holly and scream, "That's how it's done!" in his direction like some lunatic fan who's been following the team for a lifetime.

As if in slow motion, Roman twists to face us, and then

two fingers of his gloved hand extend to us, and I swear his eyes lock on mine. I freeze in place, my world narrowing to only this moment and only this man as my heart threatens to explode in my chest.

"Look! Oh my god, look!" Hannah shouts just as Holly gasps, "You're on the jumbotron!" and they both crowd around me. But my eyes stay on Roman until he finally has to drop his hand before his teammates knock him on his ass.

I realize then that I've learned three things today. One, hockey is *hot*. Two, I should never again underestimate our children, especially when it comes to meddling. And three, Roman LaFontaine doesn't appear to be done with me after all.

Chapter Thirty

Roman

We won, two-one, which is one hell of a way to go into this public announcement. I'm more nervous about Olivia's reaction than the damn game I just played, which tells me something about where my head is these days. The guys are celebrating our win while I throw my pads and helmet on the bench in the locker room. Someone claps me on the back and I turn to see Kent Bowman, our head coach. His tie is askew like it always is after he's yanked on it a thousand times in a game. Kent's always believed in me as a player who could contribute to the team, but I saw a flash of relief on his face earlier this week when I told him I'd be officially announcing my retirement after tonight's game.

"Sure this is what you want?" he asks quietly.

The fact that he's giving me a chance to forget all about my retirement plans makes me respect him more. He could use my salary next year to get two young kids in here, maybe with slightly less talent and experience, but faster skates and fewer injuries that would keep them in more games than me.

I shoot him a smile that doesn't show any of the nerves that are buzzing around in my gut. "The game schedule is really hampering my social life, Kent."

He snorts. "Yeah, like you boys need more of a social life."

It's true. We somehow always find time for closing down a bar on the road or meeting women at every hotel we stay at. The difference is now that sounds like a terrible time. I want lazy Sundays poolside with Olivia. Nights making dinner together. Holidays with all the kids. I want to hear about her day making celebrity shoes, not Banks's latest conquest.

I shake Kent's hand and he steps out of the way for me to get back out there. I run a hand through my sweaty hair and hope I'm presentable enough for this. Without delaying further, I walk back out rinkside to join Damon Whitley standing in front of a microphone and a handful of reporters that Jim vetted ahead of time.

Olivia and the kids are still in their seats. The stands usually clear out right after a game, with only the die-hard fans staying to watch the Zamboni do its thing. I grab the microphone and take a deep breath before addressing the reporters.

"Thank you for staying a bit longer. I'll get right to the point as I'm sure you have dinner plans that don't include my ugly mug." The reporters laugh, which I knew they would. You don't make it this long in a professional sport without learning how to work a crowd, but the reporters aren't the ones I'm hoping to impress tonight.

"I'm officially announcing my retirement from profes-sional hockey." My voice echoes throughout the arena. The reporters start to shout questions, but I ignore them all. "I will continue through the end of the season, and you can bet your ass, I intend for the Storm Chasers to win the cup this year."

A cheer goes up behind me and I look over my shoulder to see at least half my team piling up in the tunnel for my announcement instead of doing their own post-game interviews like they should. A warm glow that has nothing to do with skating for an hour fills my chest. I love those fuckers, believe it or not.

I swallow hard over the emotion that somehow snuck up on me. "I've accepted a head coaching position at Blue Ridge University in North Carolina. I look forward to building and developing that program into the best in the nation." When I called Hannah last night with the news I'd be joining her university, she was ecstatic rather than horrified, the reaction I'd been hoping for.

Looking up at the seats I tried like hell to ignore while I played, I lock eyes with Olivia. She has her hand over her mouth, so apparently Hannah kept the secret like I asked. "I've decided that there are other mountains to climb in hockey and I'm ready for a new challenge. In fact, I'm sure you've heard some rumors about my love life this week too."

Olivia's eyes go wide and I grin, knowing she's going to smack my arm for bringing all this attention to her. But I can't help it. A guy only professes his love for the first time once, so I have to do it right.

"Olivia Wylder, can you come on down here?" The reporters spin, excitement buzzing through the small crowd. Two of the cameramen try to get a shot of Olivia, knowing that love stories sell like hotcakes. Holly, Hannah, and Dylan tag team, getting Olivia out of her seat and taking the stairs down to this level. The security guys give me a subtle head nod. I told them before the game what would happen and even showed them pictures of Olivia like a lovesick fool so they'd know who to allow through security.

I pass off the microphone to Damon and step aside, letting him speak to the reporters about the new coaching position and what this means for his athletics department. All my attention is on the woman who already has my heart.

There she is, our kids by her side and her big eyes filling with tears. She looks even better than I remembered all week when I closed my eyes and thought back to our vacation together. I'd be a complete dumbass to think I could live without her, just flying in here and there for a visit when our schedules aligned. It isn't just the great sex—though that's spectacular and life altering all on its own. It's about envisioning a whole new chance at a life with Olivia by my side. I can see it now and I want that vision so badly I'm willing to humiliate myself on every social media platform that will run clips of this retirement announcement over and over again.

"Olivia." I didn't intend to breathe her name out loud like that, but it's like my whole body is relaxing for the first time since she walked away from me at the airport.

"Holy shit. Is that her? I love a hot cougar."

I hear Bobby behind me and have to grit my teeth when he moves up next to me. The guy has never been particularly good at reading the room.

He takes one step in Olivia's direction and I react, reaching for the microphone stand and whipping it out in front of his shins. Bobby stops on a dime, slowly turning his head to gape at me. Damon shakes his head at my antics, and several of the reporters chuckle.

"Get the fuck out of here," I growl, hoping the microphone didn't pick up that part.

He raises his hands and eyebrows equally, backing up and letting me do my thing without him stealing my spotlight.

"Total slashing penalty," I hear him grumble. The boys all give him shit, but I don't have time to waste.

"Olivia," I say again, handing the microphone stand back to Damon and stepping closer. "We didn't get a chance to say goodbye at the airport, and now I can see why. You and I aren't meant to say goodbye. If you'll let me, I believe we're just getting started."

Olivia lets out a whimper. I take her hand and step so close all she can see is me because the reporters and my fellow players don't matter. "I was going to beg to date you long distance, but I can't do it. I need to see you every day. I want to play cards at one in the morning and rip more sleeves off your dresses. I need to hear your awful singing in the shower to start my mornings. I want holiday dinners with our kids and lazy workouts and dancing in the kitchen. I want a whole life with you, Ollie. I love you."

Olivia sucks in a breath, the tears in her eyes spilling over onto her cheeks. With my free hand, I reach up and swipe them away. She leans into my hand, closing her eyes briefly like she's memorizing my touch.

"I love you too, Roman," she says softly, her gaze now burning into mine. "I didn't intend to, but I definitely do."

I smirk, more relieved than I've ever been that she feels the same way. "I'm kind of irresistible like that."

Ollie snorts while Hannah whispers something about sticking to the speech.

"I'll be moving to North Carolina after the season. Will you date me? In state and all the time?"

Olivia goes up on her tiptoes and puts her arms around my neck. My hands settle on her hips and everything about our bodies touching feels right. "I will, but only if you win that Stanford Cup first."

I frown, even as I'm smiling. "Stanley Cup?"

Olivia grins. "Sure. Whatever."

I dip my head and whisper against her lips. "You gotta come to some more games if you're going to date a hockey legend, honey."

"You got it, my Ice Bath King" she whispers back.

I lean in that extra inch, letting our lips collide and bodies press together. Everything else fades and all I feel is Olivia, my other half, my future. Her tongue is in my mouth and I have an indecent erection straining my hockey pants when the kids break us apart with their excited squeals and whistles. I blink and realize we aren't alone. Olivia's cheeks heat to a rosy pink, and I almost need to pinch myself to know that she agreed to date for real. She reaches up and swipes at my lips. I'm sure her cherry red lipstick is all over me and I couldn't give a single fuck.

"I'm usually into older women, but for you, baby, I'd make an exception." Bobby is leering at my baby girl behind my back.

My hand is already forming a fist when Banks steps in, making his long lanky body like a wall between Bobby and Hannah. "Back the fuck up before Roman rearranges your ugly face."

Olivia's eyes go wide and she puts her arm around Holly protectively. I grab Olivia's hand and reach for Hannah. "Let's get the hell out of here."

As a group, we make it down the tunnel without

further interruption from the press or my teammates. Damon already said he'd meet us at the restaurant when he was done with the press announcement.

Jim waits at the end, his hands in his trouser pockets. "Never thought I'd see the day, but love looks good on you, Roman."

I shake his hand and fasten my other arm around Olivia's waist. "Thanks to Banks, you won't have to clean up a fist fight rumor with my own teammate."

Jim rolls his eyes. "Let me guess. Bobby?"

"Can we go back and get some autographs?" Dylan asks, unable to keep quiet any longer. "Chugger would shit his pants if I got Nikolai Drugov's autograph."

"Well, we definitely don't want Chugger to shit his pants," Olivia says wryly.

"Think Banks would sign my boob?" Holly asks, earning her a death glare from Olivia.

"You are way too young, young lady!"

Holly throws up her hands. "I know! But he's still hot!"

I take control of the situation. "Ollie, you get the girls to the car. I'll take Dylan into the locker room so he can get autographs and I can get dressed. Then we have dinner reservations at eight."

"We do?" Olivia asks, forgetting about Holly and her misplaced attraction.

I lean down and kiss her quick. "Get ready. You're about to get the Roman LaFontaine full press."

Her eyes go hazy and I intend to keep putting that look on her face for years to come. "I can't wait."

<h1 style="text-align:center">Chapter Thirty-One</h1>

Olivia

"This place feels like you," Roman says as he scans my kitchen and open-plan living space, squeezing my hand—the same one he hasn't stopped holding all night.

"I'm glad you think so. I must confess I had a little help, but I've added my own touches." The place isn't exactly feminine, but it's homey and warm, just the vibe I was going for. The last thing I want is for people to walk into my house and feel like they can't touch anything or make themselves at home.

"Let me guess, the plants and the geode collection are all you." He winks, and I respond with a smile because of course he's right.

"And don't forget the dish towels." I gesture to my oven door where two matching flour-sack towels hang, one declaring, "If cauliflower can be pizza, you can be anything," and the second, "Cupcakes are muffins that believed in miracles."

He yanks on my hand to pull me in for a kiss, and I murmur against his lips, "Thanks for tonight, Ice Bath King."

I feel his lips curve up before he lays a hot and heavy one on me.

Dinner with Roman, Damon, and the kids was an absolute blast, especially with both of us riding the high of his very public stunt at the arena. I still can't believe he's not only retiring but moving to North Carolina, something I'll be pinching myself over for weeks, I'm certain. He took us to my favorite cozy Italian spot, Ever Andalo, in NoDa, which he somehow remembered me mentioning in passing while we were in Belize. I told you, he's magic.

Afterwards, we bid farewell to Damon—who I immediately liked—and Dylan drove the girls back to BRU, once they promised to keep him from nodding off at the wheel after that big meal, that is. Honestly, I didn't try too hard to keep them with us overnight when Roman informed me he was staying over at my place. Cue whole body shiver.

"Why don't you show me your underwear collection next?" Roman asks.

My body shakes with laughter at his poorly hidden agenda, but he doesn't need to ask me twice before I lead him up the stairs. He gets the abbreviated tour along the way, but I don't know why I bother since his eyes never leave my backside the whole way to my bedroom.

Feeling bold from our declarations of love, I pause at the edge of the bed, then turn and push Roman back a few feet. He clocks my naughty grin immediately and stays put, eyes raking my body from head to toe. My hands drop to the hem of my sweater and I whip it off in one fluid motion before tackling my jeans. My eyes never leave his, so I spot the exact moment they go from lazy to fiery, and it just happens to coincide with the very second I lose my bra.

But I don't get the chance to rid myself of my lace and satin panties—a girl's always got to be prepared, right?—before he's on me and taking me down to the bed. I lift my head to crush my lips to his, and it takes about a third of a second for Roman to take control of the kiss. I grin against his lips, and he uses the opportunity to slip his tongue between my teeth. My tongue meets his stroke for stroke and everything south of my navel bursts into flame.

My fingers twist in his hair as I begin to pant into his mouth. With a surge of self-assurance and good old-fashioned horniness, I flip us so I'm on top and lift up to straddle his thighs. His smile tells me I only managed that maneuver because he let me, but the smile drops as soon as I reach up to cup my own naked breasts.

"Fuck, you're hot," he says on a growl, and I feel the rumble from his chest in my clit.

"Right back atcha, LaFontaine," I respond, pulling his shirt from his pants as he grabs my ass with both hands and squeezes. Hard. As soon as I reveal his bare skin with its smattering of chest hair and variety of faded scars, I slide down his body to have a taste. He's all firmness and heat with skin that's salty on my tongue.

Roman sheds his shirt entirely, and I return to my sensory exploration of his chest and stomach, flicking my tongue down his happy trail. He groans and pulls me up by my ass cheeks so I'm straddling him again. He then draws one of my peaked nipples into his mouth, biting down gently. I moan and arch my back, silently begging for more. His tongue soothes the spot he's bitten before moving to my other breast.

By this point, his erection is pressing solidly against my

core, so he shifts me to quickly rid himself of the rest of his clothes before sliding his hands into my panties in a silent command for me to do the same. I'm not about to argue.

When we're both fully naked, his eyes devour me and my usual flush spreads over my entire body. I don't know if it's lust or a hot flash, but what I know it's *not* is self-consciousness. Because Roman's eyes hold nothing but lust and affection.

He loves me. And I love him. And that's all there is to it.

His fingertips gently caress me from the tops of my breasts down to my knees, those fiery whiskey eyes following his hands the entire time. I feel beautiful and feminine and...worshipped. It's a heady sensation and one I know he'll keep giving me as we build a life together.

When he finally lifts his eyes to mine again, his voice is a hoarse whisper. "You are so goddamn beautiful, Olivia." Then he takes my mouth again and we get down to business for real.

We're a frenetic tumble of limbs and mouths, each of us exploring every square inch of the other's body. At one point, I nearly fall off the bed, but Roman catches me at the last second with a move that has him groaning—in pain this time. However, my expressed concern over his condition is only met with a cocky, "Even with one good arm, I can still fuck you hard like you need it," as only my man could deliver.

Suffice it to say, I shut my mouth and let him get on with it. And when my orgasm takes me higher than I've ever gone before, I have my proof that Roman LaFontaine is indeed an MVP both on and off the ice.

Not that I ever needed more evidence.

"Okay, Olivia, now turn to the side. Yes, just like that," the photographer instructs, and I do my best to comply. The shutter clicks in a staccato beat as he smiles at me from behind his giant camera. To my utter surprise, the Style-Wire photo shoot is kind of a rush. Who knew?

Roman, of course, assisted with my wardrobe selection, in addition to copping more than a few feels while I modeled potential outfits for him. Despite his desire to be here today and cheer me on, duty called and he had to head back to Tampa for a home game. The team is looking great, and he assures me they'll make the playoffs. When they do, I'll be right there cheering him on.

The reporter from StyleWire interviewed me this morning. From our first introduction, she and I clicked, chatting easily about everything from airport travel to kids leaving the nest to menopause fog-brain. She even recommended a top menopause specialist in New York who just happens to be the same one Roman found for me through his connections only last week. I'm seriously considering getting my butt on a plane to find what relief is out there, if any exists.

The interview itself went off without a hitch. She'd heard about Roman and me, of course, but the focus was entirely about me and my experiences combining technology with fashion to build a unique brand. I remained upfront, giving due fashion credit to Ashley and our design team, which I recently expanded to give myself more breathing room.

After our sit-down, I took her on a tour of our facility,

showing off our print studio and giving her a brief glimpse of our top-secret scanning technology. I also made it a point to send her Ashley's way, which had my assistant nearly vibrating with excitement. We parted having exchanged numbers and a promise to meet up for lunch if I end up going to NYC.

I can't wait to read the final feature when it's done.

"Okay, with the earlier shots and these, I think we've got everything we need, Olivia," the photographer straightens from a squat and smiles my way.

I rise from my spot on the chaise in my office to shake his hand. "Thank you so much, Allesandro."

He and his team pack up and disappear in no time, giving me my first chance to touch base with Roman today.

"Hey, honey." His greeting and the warmth in his tone have me sighing. "How did it go?"

"Honestly, amazing," I share, relaxing back into the chaise again and peeling my cropped raspberry jacket from my shoulders. Then I tell Roman all about my day.

"Sounds like you knocked it out of the park."

"Wrong sport. Maybe it *is* time to retire," I tease. "How was practice?"

"Another day, another reminder that I'm getting out just in time." I can hear the exhaustion in his tone.

"Aw, I wish I was there to feel you up—oops, I mean, give you a massage."

His responding chuckle in my ear has my belly warming, so I continue, "I'll make it up to you on Sunday after we go apartment hunting."

Roman and I have worked out a routine these past few weeks, with him staying in Charlotte whenever he can and me flying down to Tampa when my schedule allows. It's been hectic but exhilarating, and I can't wait until his season is over and he officially moves to North Carolina.

Not that I haven't been enjoying my newfound fandom of all things hockey. Okay, well it might have more to do with how hot my man is on the ice, but either way, I'm all in.

With Roman's new job at BRU starting immediately after the season is over, he plans to put his place in Tampa on the market and temporarily move into an apartment somewhere closer to BRU while we make sure our future is rock solid. And with campus only a little over an hour from my house, it will be a hell of a lot easier to see each other once he moves.

"About that," he murmurs, and I can perfectly picture his naughty grin even from hundreds of miles away. "Hannah called last night, and we had a long chat."

This is not where I thought he was going. "What about?" I hold the phone between my ear and shoulder while I pin my hair up to get it off my neck.

"It was really more of a lecture than a talk, now that I think about it."

I snort and wait for him to continue.

"She thinks we should skip the apartment and dive straight in, and I'm thinking she's right. Why waste time when we both already know where we're going?"

My back straightens at his words, and a liquid warmth spreads through my chest. "You want to move in with me?" I ask on a breathy exhale, gripping the phone firmly to my ear now.

"Yeah, Ollie, I wanna move in with you."

I feel my face get soft before my lips widen into a smile. "Well, that's awfully convenient since I want that too." But I still have to ask, "Are you sure the drive won't be too much? Honestly, I'd move to a halfway spot in a heartbeat if it meant having you sleeping next to me every night." My confession is honest and immediate because this is Roman, and there's no reason to hide my feelings.

"I can hack it," he responds, "especially if it means having your sweet ass in my hands at the end of the day."

"You really are the king of romance, aren't you, LaFontaine?" I tease.

"Just wait until Sunday and you'll find out."

I'm sure I will, so my smile broadens. "Okay, Roman. We'll talk more tonight. Right now, I've got to run."

"Got a meeting, boss lady?"

"Nope," I reply. "I've got to buy my guy some blankets before he moves in."

The last thing I hear before hanging up is Roman's deep, rumbling laughter, and it cuts right through me to settle in the center of my heart.

Epilogue

Roman

Olivia thinks we opened all the gifts last night with the kids, but while she sings an off-key rendition of "Rudolph the Red Nosed Reindeer" in the shower, I slide one last present under the Christmas tree. The last few months have been better than I could have ever dreamed, living together and sharing our daily lives, surrounded by our families. Only one more thing would make it perfect, and I intend to take care of that this morning.

When Olivia comes into the living room with her wet hair piled on top of her head and sporting the Wilcox Wombat hockey pajamas I got her for Christmas, not because I have any affiliation with the team but because I knew Olivia would love them (little wombats holding hockey sticks, you can't beat it), I motion her to join me on the couch.

I hand her the cup of coffee I poured for her–decaf–and she sends me an appreciative look. "I can't get over how many presents we opened last night! The kids already have everything they need."

I shrug and open my mouth, but she beats me to it.

"I know, I know. What's the point of making all this money if you can't spend it on the people you love."

"I may have retired from playing, but this old man's still got plenty of endorsements, even if they're for painkillers and muscle creams instead of sports drinks now." I wave away that direction of thought. "But speaking of the people I love," I drawl, standing up. My knee doesn't even scream at me thanks to less skating and more yoga since retirement from the league. "I have one last gift for you."

"Roman!" She clinks her coffee cup down on the table beside the couch. "You already got me season tickets to the Silverkings and a new car. I really don't need anything!"

That sensible white Volvo most certainly needed replacing with a Porsche SUV, but I'll leave that argument for another day. I shoot her a wink and head over to the Christmas tree. Having set this up ahead of time, I already have my battered high school hockey stick leaning against the wall. I grab it, assuming an exaggerated stance.

"You are mistaken, m'lady. We may have won the Stanley Cup this year, and I may have scored my share of the points that got us there, but this is my most important shot yet." With a deft flick of the wrist, I send the black velvet box sailing across the wooden floors.

Olivia's bare feet catch the box with reflexes that rival Niko's. She swoops down and picks it up, her eyebrows winging up on her forehead. "What is this?"

When I get down on my good knee in front of her, Olivia finally catches up. Her eyes instantly fill with tears but her mouth is grinning ear to ear. Joy looks good on her.

I put my hands over hers to crack open the box and

show off the ridiculously huge diamond I got for her, because literally nothing smaller would have been adequate to be a representation of my love. And because I want her to know she deserves all the best things in life.

"Olivia, you came into my life like a dozen slashes straight to the chest," I start, earning myself a snort, "Disrupting everything I thought I wanted for my future. Everything came to a screeching halt and you gave me the space to examine my choices. The first half of my life was great, but it took meeting you to realize that I was clinging to something that was no longer serving me. Being here with you, the kids, this life together in North Carolina...it's brought me to my knees. Literally."

Olivia hiccups back a sob. "Roman."

"Shh. Not done yet. I didn't even have the kids help me with this speech." I squeeze her hands. "I want to be all that and more for you. I want to be the man you lean on, the one who will lift you up, and encourage you to see yourself as you truly are: incredible, talented, and so damn worthy of everything in this life, no matter what age you are. I want to grow older with you. I want to fan your face every time you get a hot flash. I want to see you build a fashion empire with your incredible brain. I want to hold our grandkids together in this house and wipe the happy tears from your cheeks. I want to love you with every single one of the breaths I have left. Will you marry me, honey?"

Olivia presses her lips together, a single tear from each eye leaking down her face. She taps the back of my hands, and I know she just needs a minute. I'll give her a thousand. Thankfully–because even my good knee is starting to send up an SOS–she doesn't need that many.

"Yes," she whispers, clears her throat and tries again. "Yes!"

I don't wait for her to change her mind on a broken-down ex-hockey player. I get to my feet and bring her with me. Our lips crash together and now the holidays are truly magical. Olivia hitches her leg over my hip and I grab a handful of that ass that never fails to make me hornier than the eighteen-year-old boys on my new college hockey team.

Reluctantly, I pull away just enough to take the ring out of the box. "Slow down a second, honey. Next time I sink into your body I want to see my ring on your finger."

"Possessive, are we?" she asks with plenty of sass.

"Damn right, I am." I slide the ring on her finger and we both pause to watch it sparkle in the multi-colored lights from the tree.

"It's beautiful, Roman, but this life with you is even more beautiful." Olivia looks up at me and everything clicks into place. I'm exactly where I was always meant to be. Every road trip across the country over the last two decades led me right here to this woman's doorstep in North Carolina.

I waggle my eyebrows. "What do you say we consummate our engagement?"

Olivia frowns. "Isn't consummating for after the wedding?"

I shrug. "This is our second half of life. I think we get to make the rules up this time."

Olivia doesn't waste a second. She jumps and I catch her, tucking her against my waist as I stumble to our bedroom. The trek is perhaps a little slower than it would have been in my younger days, but we make it, and the love making is better than ever.

"I can't believe you answered the door with a hickey on your neck," Banks drawls, swirling the whiskey in his glass as he pounds the appetizers Olivia spent all day making, even when I tried to distract her with coming back to bed. It had been my idea to have Christmas dinner with some of my hockey friends, considering our kids were all with their other parents for Christmas Day. I'm already reconsidering this plan.

"You should try a monogamous relationship for once in your life. It has all kinds of side benefits."

Banks shivers. "No, thanks."

Olivia comes into the living room with another tray of those little sandwiches that Banks, Niko, and Bobby already managed to devour within ten minutes of arriving. I leap up to help her and ignore Banks's quiet laughter. He has no idea what he's missing.

Bobby jumps up and grabs a sandwich in each hand, leaning in to kiss Olivia's cheek. I shove him away before he can linger too long. "You're a goddess, Olivia."

"Who the fuck invited this guy?" I ask the room. Banks ignores me, Niko looks like he's ready to smash his fist through someone's face just for breathing, and Olivia back-hands my arm.

"Be nice to our guests," she whispers without any heat behind it. She's used to the amount of ribbing we engage in. Even after retiring, these guys still call me weekly to check in and catch up. Even fucking Bobby.

Despite being professional athletes, they're a bunch of

misfits. I feel like they need help with their personal lives and it's my job to step in. Maybe it's just my post-engagement bliss, but these fellas could use a good woman in their lives.

The doorbell rings and I drop a quick kiss on Olivia's lips before moving to answer it. Fashionably late like all good women are, Kaitlyn Phillips stands on my doorstep in a full-length fur coat that is surely overkill, even in winter here in Charlotte. Her smile is dazzling and I return it, just envisioning the look on Banks's face when he sees our final dinner guest.

"Kaitlyn! Come on in." She steps forward and we hug. She lets me take her coat, leaving her in a red dress that looks practically painted on. I don't bother looking because the prettiest woman I know steps into the foyer and shakes Kaitlyn's hand.

"I'm so glad you could make it!" The women hug and Olivia's smile doesn't look forced this time.

"Wouldn't miss it for the world." Kaitlyn's smile falters. "Didn't have anywhere else to be, if I'm being honest."

Olivia wraps her arm around Kaitlyn's and tugs her toward the living room. I knew Olivia would immediately take her under her wing. Olivia can't walk away from someone who needs her. "You'll feel right at home here, even if I have to beat these boys away from you with Roman's hockey stick."

Kaitlyn groans, but it's too late now. I purposely didn't tell her who all would be here. I follow behind the ladies, mostly to make sure Kaitlyn doesn't tuck and run when she sees Banks. Those two have never held back their contempt for one another.

"Is this a collection of Santa's naughty list or what?" Kaitlyn drawls, surveying the room.

Banks leaps to his feet and slams his glass down on the table next to him. "And you must be the lump of coal in my stocking."

"Banks! Sit your ass down right now or I will charge you a grand for each of the sandwiches you just ate," Olivia snaps. Banks immediately sinks back down to the couch obediently. I've never been so proud of Olivia. "Kaitlyn is my guest and you all will be kind to her, even if I have to tape your mouth shut. Are we clear?"

Banks nods but he looks like he swallowed a lemon. Bobby grins like this is the best shit he's ever seen.

"Yes, ma'am," Nico replies solemnly.

Dinner goes off without a hitch and we even get Banks to contribute to the conversation here and there. Kaitlyn licks her lips and runs her fingers along the edge of her wine glass just to make Banks squirm. I have no idea why they hate each other, but I have a feeling, given enough time, they might find a way to see eye to eye. Nico leans over to mumble his life story to Olivia. I don't hear much of it, but I do catch that he's sad to not have his daughter during the holidays. He's in a court battle with his ex-wife and from the quick swipes to the corner of her eyes while Nico tells Olivia his story, I can tell it's not going well. Bobby keeps the conversation lively on the other end of the table, and for once, I welcome his constant humor. It's over dessert that everything goes to hell.

"I heard your agent dropped you," Kaitlyn purrs, looking directly at Banks.

My fork clinks to the plate. He hadn't told me that.

Banks looks like he wants to wrap his hands around Kaitlyn's neck and give it a firm squeeze. He throws his napkin down on the table and shrugs. "I'll find another. Or negotiate it myself."

Kaitlyn scoffs. "Negotiate your own contract at thirty-eight years old? The team is probably trying to get rid of you. If anything, you'll need one hell of an agent to keep you skating, hot shot."

"None of your concern," he fires back.

"You could just fall in love and retire like me," I suggest, reaching over to hold Olivia's hand.

Banks and Kaitlyn both grimace right on cue.

"I'd rather move my shit right into an old folk's home." Banks dips his head to Olivia. "No offense to our fabulous host, of course. There's just not many women out there like you."

"He's allergic to love." Kaitlyn smirks, taking a sip of wine.

"Says the woman who isn't brave enough to even get near it." Banks's smirk is even smirkier.

I scrape my chair back. My patience has run out and these assholes need to take their ba-humbug attitude somewhere else. "Thank you all for coming, but you can leave now."

"Roman!" Olivia hisses.

"What? We just got engaged this morning. Surely they can understand that we'd like a little alone time."

Olivia's cheeks flame pink, but she doesn't try to stop me.

"I don't know. I hear some chicks are into threesomes," Bobby interjects with a flirty wink aimed at my fiancée.

I lunge around the table to strangle the man, but he dashes away from the dining room and toward our front door. The fucker's fast. "I'm kidding, dude!" He's out the door and on the porch, still yelling over his shoulder. "Thank you, Olivia! Your home is wonderful and I've never seen Roman so happy!"

I growl at his retreating back. He flips me off but then shoots me a smile before climbing into his truck. "Seriously. Well done, Roman. I know I tease you about being an old man, but I really hope I have all the things you have when I'm your age."

"It's not the things, Bobby. It's the people." Yep, I've become the old man these days, dispensing wisdom from my front porch.

He tilts his head. "Does Olivia have a sister?"

I throw a hand through the air, waving him off. "Drive safe, loser."

"Hope you don't have a heart attack during sex, old man."

He drives off while I chuckle. Nico sneaks up behind me on the porch. The bastard is huge but quiet. "I must leave now so you can get going with the nookie."

I cringe. "No one says that."

"What? Is nookie not American for sex? Plus, those two in there are giving me a headache." He ambles down the porch steps, favoring his right leg. I'd ask about it, but I know he wouldn't want to talk about his injuries.

"I hope next Christmas we can meet your daughter."

He nods, spinning his keys in his hand. "I will move heaven and earth to have her with me all the time."

I don't bother to question how he can do that and still be on the road all the time during the season. I don't have the time to have my face bashed in. Not with my fiancée waiting for me. He leaves, a stoic frown firmly in place.

I go back inside to see Olivia wringing her hands as Banks and Kaitlyn are standing toe to toe, snarling at each other. Pushing my way between them, I get them to muzzle themselves before they shed blood on our floors.

"I thought maybe you two could chat like adults, but apparently I was wrong."

Banks points right in her face. "I don't like her."

Kaitlyn snaps her teeth like she means to bite him. "Same, hot shot, same."

Olivia gets Kaitlyn in her coat, while I yank Banks in the direction of his vehicle. Probably best to keep them separated from now on. Guess my matchmaking skills aren't as superb as my puckhandling skills.

"Why didn't you tell me about your agent?"

Banks won't meet my eyes. "Not sure what I'm going to do about it yet. Why bring it up when you're all aglow with happiness?"

I slap my hand on his shoulder. "Hey, we're more than former teammates. We're friends, Banks. Share everything with me. Maybe I can help."

Banks's gaze shifts back to the house where Olivia and Kaitlyn are saying goodbye in the doorway. "That one is definitely not helping."

I nod. "Understood. Won't happen again."

We hug with thick slaps to the back and then he's gone. I apologize to Kaitlyn but she's already laughing it off.

"He's an asshole, but he keeps my comebacks sharp." She gives me a hug. "I'm so glad I got to see the great Roman LaFontaine in his natural habitat."

She glides away to the last remaining car in our driveway while I stare up at Olivia's silhouette in the doorway. The Christmas lights all around her cast her in a festive flow. The grin is as natural as breathing. This *is* my natural habitat...home with Olivia.

I holler up to her, not giving a damn about our neighbors. "I think we have just enough time for three more hochimamas this Christmas!"

"Roman!" Her mouth drops open, but then she spins on her heel and runs into the house, stripping off her blouse. I follow, running faster than I ever skated in the league.

Stay tuned for Mood Swings and Hockey Flings, book two in the Hot Flash Hookups series...coming early 2024! In the meantime, grab a free novella from Marika here (https://dl.bookfunnel.com/9cwzbg0rqo). *And grab a freebie from Sylvie here* (http://bit.ly/s-s-nl)!

Scan the QR code to go to Marika's Amazon page!

<u>Steamy Holiday RomCom</u>

Grumpy Little Christmas - Standalone

***

<u>Steamy RomComs - Blueball Band of Brothers:</u>

Grumpy the Bear - Blueball Band of Brothers #1

S'more Than a Feeling - Blueball Band of Brothers #2

***

<u>All Steamy RomComs Set in Hell:</u>

Grumpy As Hell - Hellman Brothers #1

Bro Code Hell - Hellman Brothers #2

Friend Zone Hell - Hellman Brothers #3

Cougar From Hell - Hellman Brothers #4

Falling First Hell - Hellman Brothers #5

Matchmaker From Hell - FREE Novella

***

Ridin' Solo - Sisters From Hell #1

One Night Bride - Sisters From Hell #2

Smarty Pants - Sisters From Hell #3

Ex Best Thing - Sisters From Hell #4

***

Love Bank - Jobs From Hell #1

Uber Bossy - Jobs From Hell #2

Unfriend Me - Jobs From Hell #3

Side Hustle - Jobs From Hell #4

Man Glitter - FREE Novella

***

Backroom Boy - Standalone

Steamy RomComs:

The Missing Ingredient - Reality of Love #1

Mom-Com - Reality of Love #2

Desperately Seeking Househusbands - Reality of Love #3

Steamy Beach Romance:

1) Sweet Dreams - Beach Squad #1

2) Love on the Defense - Beach Squad #2

3) Barefoot Chaos - Beach Squad #3

* Novella - Handcuffed Hussy

4) Beach Babe Billionaire- Beach Squad #4

5) Brighter Than the Boss - Beach Squad #5

* Novella - Christmas Eve Do-Over

SCAN ME

Ale's Fair in Love and War (*Love on Tap*, Book 1)

Smooth Hoperator (*Love on Tap*, Book 2)

Deja Brew All Over Again (*Love on Tap*, Book 3)

Asheville Collection (Standalone Stories from the *Love on Tap* World)

* * *

The Fix (*Carolina Connections*, Book 1)

The Spark (*Carolina Connections*, Book 2)

The Lucky One (*Carolina Connections*, Book 3)

The Game (*Carolina Connections*, Book 4)

The Way You Are (*Carolina Connections*, Book 5)

The Runaround (*Carolina Connections*, Book 6)
Carolina Connections Box Set 1
Carolina Connections Box Set 2

* * *

The Nerd Next Door (*Carolina Kisses*, Book 1)
New Jerk in Town (*Carolina Kisses*, Book 2)
The Last Good Liar (*Carolina Kisses*, Book 3)

* * *

Between a Rock and a Royal, *Kings of Carolina, #1*
Blue Bloods and Backroads, *Kings of Carolina, #2*
Stealing Kisses With a King, *Kings of Carolina, #3*
Kings of Carolina Box Set

* * *

Poppy & the Beast
Then Again

Full-On Clinger (FREE for a limited time)
About That
Nuts About You
Booby Trapped

Acknowledgments

Marika and Sylvie met years ago at a book signing, instantly hitting it off as they were both quite funny. Fast forward a few years and they were on the phone lamenting all the very real symptoms of peri menopause that were affecting their lives when they both had the grand idea that they wanted to write about it! The goal was to normalize conversation about the various side effects of the hormonal rollercoaster that is aging, while also reminding women of their inherent beauty no matter their age.

From Sylvie - A personal thanks to Allison, Carlie, and Annette for their support, and to my trusty neck fan for pulling me through my worst hot flashes.

From Marika - A big huge thank you to my husband, not only for his understanding, but also his patience when I yell at him for having the audacity to fall asleep so fast when I can't anymore. And his chewing. Dear god, the man's chewing!

Thank you to fellow romance authors for their enthusiasm and support of this book. You make a girl feel less crazy.

Last but not least...a huge thank you to Nancy Smay at Evident Ink for making this book shine with your editing and proofreading services!

About Marika Ray

Marika Ray is a USA Today bestselling author, writing small town RomCom to make your heart explode and bring a smile to your face. All her books come with a money-back guarantee that you'll laugh at least once with every book.

Marika spends her time behind a computer crafting stories, walking along the beach, and making healthy food for her kids and husband whether they like it or not. Prior to writing novels, Marika held various jobs in the finance industry, with private start-up companies, and then in health & fitness. Cats may have nine lives, but Marika believes everyone should have nine careers to keep things spicy.

If you'd like to know more about Marika or the other novels she's currently writing, please find her at www.marikaray.com.

If you want to take your stalking to the next level, here are other legal (ish) places you can find Marika:

Join her Newsletter - http://bit.ly/MarikaRayNews

Amazon - https://www.amazon.com/author/marikaray

Goodreads - https://www.goodreads.com/author/show/16856659.Marika_Ray

Bookbub - https://www.bookbub.com/authors/marika-ray

TikTok - https://vm.tiktok.com/ZMJvnQ2Cv

Instagram - https://www.instagram/authormarikaray

About Sylvie Stewart

USA Today bestselling author Sylvie Stewart loves dad jokes, dirty rom-coms, country music, and baby skunks—preferably all at the same time. Most of her steamy contemporary and romantic comedy novels take place across her favorite state of North Carolina, and her characters never run out of snarky banter or snacks. When her laptop closes, Sylvie is a sucker for hugs from her twin boys and a good laugh with her hot-nerd hubby. If you love smart Southern gals, hot blue-collar guys, and snort-laughing with characters who feel like your best friends, Sylvie's your gal. Stay up to date on all things Sylvie! https://sylviestewartauthor.com

Join her Newsletter - http://bit.ly/s-s-nl

Facebook Reader Group - https://www.facebook.com/groups/743238732533487

Facebook Page — https://facebook.com/SylvieStewartAuthor

Instagram — https://instagram.com/sylvie.stewart.romance

BookBub — https://bookbub.com/authors/sylvie-stewart

Twitter — https://twitter.com/sylvie_stewart_

TikTok – https://tiktok.com/@authorsylviestewart

Pinterest – https://pinterest.com/sylviestewartauthor

Goodreads – https://goodreads.com/author/show/
15303783.Sylvie_Stewart

YouTube – https://youtube.com/@sylviestewartauthor

www.ingramcontent.com/pod-product-compliance
Lightning Source LLC
Chambersburg PA
CBHW020752190726
48285CB00006B/1995